"I INTEND TO BECOME INDEPENDENT."

Ashtead frowned. "In what way?"

"In *every* way!" Eddie exclaimed. "You are a man. You can have no idea what it is like to be wholly independent for *everything*. I won't be forced to go somewhere, or to do something, or to marry simply because it pleases someone else that I should. I want to be able to say no if I wish to."

"We all of us must do things from time to time that we would rather not," he pointed out.

She fixed him with a reproving stare. "If my grandfather were to cast you off right now, where would you sleep this night? From where would you get your next meal? You have your own properties. You are not wholly dependent upon the whims of another."

"No. But what." he said slowly, "has that to say to your playing piquet with that profligate?"

"Everything." She looked up at him from beneath partially lowered lashes. "Can you not see? I *will* be independent. The only way to achieve that is by securing a competence."

He stared at her for a long moment while the significance of her words sank home. "Do you mean to say you hope to *win* this independence of yours?"

Other books by Janice Bennett

Regencies:

AN ELIGIBLE BRIDE
TANGLED WEB
MIDNIGHT MASQUE
AN INTRIGUING DESIRE
A TEMPTING KISS
A LOGICAL LADY
A LADY'S CHAMPION
THE MATCHMAKING GHOST
THE CANDLELIGHT WISH
THE STARLIGHT WISH
THE MOONLIGHT WISH

Regency Mysteries:
A MYSTERIOUS MISS
A DANGEROUS INTRIGUE
A DESPERATE GAMBLE

Time Travels:
A TIMELY AFFAIR
FOREVER IN TIME
A CHRISTMAS KEEPSAKE
A TOUCH OF FOREVER
ACROSS FOREVER

Futuristic:
AMETHYST MOON

Published by Zebra Books and Pinnacle Books

THE MOONLIGHT WISH

Janice Bennett

Zebra Books
Kensington Publishing Corp.

http://www.zebrabooks.com

ZEBRA BOOKS are published by

Kensington Publishing Corp.
850 Third Avenue
New York, NY 10022

First Printing: June, 2000
10 9 8 7 6 5 4 3 2 1

Printed in the United States of America

For all of you, especially those of you who have written to me over the years. Thank you.

Prologue

The fairy, a comfortable being of humorous aspect, hovered three feet above the clover-strewn meadow, sitting cross-legged in midair, her expression one of intense concentration as she listened to the musical trilling that filled the warm summer morning. Before her, on a row of hollyhocks, perched a dozen canaries, their heads tilted back in glorious song. Xanthe hummed a measure along with them, gestured with the twig of plum wood she held in her hand for a baton, and half a dozen meadowlarks swooped down to take their places in the avian choir, adding their sweet voices to the melody. That was more like it; she liked the counterpoint. Her set of double oval wings began beating gently, keeping time. A single round feather, transparent except for its golden tip, fluttered to the ground.

She pushed back the long sleeves of her green tunic, which hung in graceful folds about her plump figure. A few strands of her long golden hair escaped the thick braids that looped about her head. Tiny violets fastened the plaits at strategic points, and more of the delicately scented blossoms floated about her, clinging to the soft fabric of her skirt, trailing along her slippers. She loved summer. But then she also loved autumn, winter, and spring.

A flock of robins landed amongst the canaries and meadowlarks, causing the birds to shuffle their positions with a fluttering of wings and the missing of a few notes. Before they had properly settled, a number of exuberant orioles and sparrows swept through, accompanied by four herring gulls, three macaws, two flamingos, and an ostrich. Xanthe blinked, regarding her oddly assorted but enthusiastic choir as each bird caroled forth with its own peculiar—and highly discordant—song.

The fairy closed her eyes. "Titus," she said in tones of amused resignation.

A huge white cat materialized in one of the lower branches of an apple tree. He blinked sleepy eyes, his expression smug. But since that was a feline's ordinary manner of staring at people, it gave nothing away.

Xanthe sighed. "Vexatious beast," she said, but without heat. She was hardly guiltless herself of the art of playing mischievous jokes on her assistant. Like the time she had filled the kitchen with mice that danced a Scottish reel, then transformed into a cricket orchestra, complete with euphoniums and bassoons. Titus had hardly flicked an ear at her all that afternoon, until he retaliated that evening by inviting a clan of pixies to picnic in her bed. The sleepy fairy had bowed gracefully to the inevitable, shrunk both herself and Titus to the size of their guests, and they'd all passed a merry night.

A peacock blinked into existence before her, spread his magnificent tail with a snap, then strutted before the other birds, screeching its banshee cry. Xanthe allowed herself to settle to the fragrant grass. Another of her rounded feathers drifted lazily to the green carpet at her feet. "I take it you wanted me for something," she said to Titus.

The massive cat flicked the tip of his bushy tail.

Xanthe brightened. "Really? Why didn't you say so at once? What did you see?"

Slowly the cat's eyes closed, then opened once more. In the depths of his pupils glowed tiny cream-colored spheres, mottled with shadows.

"Moons," Xanthe breathed, and her smile widened. "Oh, how delightful. Let us go back immediately."

She hurried across the forest-lined meadow, back through the trellised gate with its pale pink roses climbing and cascading over the bent wood frame, then followed the paving-stone walkway between shrubs of flowering lavender and lilacs. A flight of butterflies flitted about her, then swooped down to land upon the cat, who ran lightly ahead. Xanthe stepped from the early summer heat into the cool interior of her kitchen, then across the flagged stone floor to the room that served both as her dining and living area.

The window stood open, its lace curtains stirring gently in the soft breeze. Half a dozen feather dusters plied themselves about the furnishings, but she dismissed them with a single hummed bar as she made her way to the mahogany sideboard, on which rested a shallow silver basin, its exterior chased with a pattern of oak and ivy leaves. About it stood four thick beeswax candles set in holders that matched the bowl. Water filled the mirrored interior, which at the moment reflected a full moon riding in a velvet sky, just above a shadowy line of trees.

"Moonlight," Xanthe murmured.

She pulled open the top drawer of the sideboard, then studied the oddly assorted contents. Star-shaped candleholders she pushed aside, along with several crystals of varying hues. Nor did she need the herb-stuffed sachets. Her hand hesitated over a carved malachite box, then moved on to a velvet pouch from which she poured an assortment of polished chunks of amber, jade, jet, and turquoise. She tumbled these back into their bag and selected another pouch. From this one she drew a four-inch sphere of moonstone and held it up to the light, a smile of triumph just touching her lips. "Moonlight," she repeated.

A hummed bar of music sent it floating to hover above the basin. Titus sprang lightly to the lace-topped worktable, then eased his magnificent bulk across the two-foot span to the sideboard. He positioned himself over the bowl so that Xanthe had to boost him gently aside in order to see inside herself.

Titus turned his nose toward her and blinked.

"I am well aware of it," the fairy informed him.

She rummaged through the drawer once more and came out with three clear crystal spheres, which she sent circling the one of moonstone. Another hummed bar caused the candles to burst into flame. She leaned forward, stroking the cat's fur, as he set up a rhythmic purring in counterpoint to her soft humming.

After a moment, she passed a hand over the basin, and the waters began to stir as if moved by a breeze. Light refracted from the surface, replayed by the mirrors on the interior so that it danced and sparkled about the walls of the room. The motion of the water quickened; tiny wavelets formed, then roiled about the bowl, bubbling and swirling until they formed a whirlpool, which drew the gaze down into the shallow depth as if it were a bottomless ocean. Mists formed, obscuring the basin, then drifted and parted as Xanthe passed her hand over the surface once more. The roiling slowed, then stilled, and Xanthe and Titus gazed at the image revealed within.

A young woman stared toward them, as if she looked through a window but could not see what lay beyond the glass. Large gray eyes gazed sadly into nothingness from above a straight nose. The mouth appeared just a shade too wide for perfect beauty, the chin was a trifle square and stubborn, and the expression bespoke a mingling unhappiness and fear that wrenched at Xanthe's heart. Long straight hair of a soft brown color smoothed back from the girl's face, though a few strands escaped from the chignon at the base of her neck. A shabby pelisse of dull brown merino covered an outmoded evening gown of pale blue muslin.

"To look at her," Xanthe said, "you would never know she was heiress to a vast fortune, would you?"

Titus emitted a noise that sounded like *eck*.

"What? Oh." Xanthe paused for a moment, allowing her thoughts to envelope that unhappy girl. "Lady Edwina Langston. She's the granddaughter of the Marquis of Shoreham, the daughter of his only son. Poor child, she is just discovering how very little say she may have in her own destiny."

Titus directed a penetrating stare at the fairy.

Xanthe laughed. "Naturally. We shall see that she has a great deal of say." She regarded the dejected face a moment longer. "How very lonely and confused she is. What?" she added, directing a quelling look at the cat, who made a show of licking a paw and straightening a whisker. "I never dictate to people. I only grant them opportunities to discover their heart's desire."

Titus stopped his ablutions and blinked at her.

"Well, and what if they do need a little help? Humans always seem to make such a muddle of their affairs. And if they didn't, where would that leave us?"

The tip of one white ear twitched.

Xanthe shook her head. "You'd be bored, my dear, and well you know it."

A rumbling purr sounded deep in the cat's throat.

Xanthe laughed. "So I should think." She hummed a lively air, and the candles extinguished themselves, the spheres danced back into their protective pouches, and within moments the drawer in the sideboard closed itself upon her treasures. The feather dusters reappeared and swept the last traces of motes and particles from the furnishings, then vanished in puffs of brightly colored smoke. The fairy looked about the tidy room and nodded in satisfaction. "There. Well, Titus, are you ready to go to work?"

One

Charles Edward Langston, Viscount Ashtead, halted before the door of his great-uncle's bedchamber and raised his hand to knock. Before his rap could fall, the heavy oak panel swung wide, revealing a frail figure with thinning hair and rheumy eyes, his features set in an expression of fatalistic moroseness. The viscount lowered his hand, his brow creasing. "Has the old gentleman really had notice to quit, Stebbings?"

The aged valet nodded his head. "Aye, though I'll not believe it till he's breathed his last, m'lord."

"Nor shall I," murmured Ashtead, and moved past the elderly man into the dark interior of the antechamber. A cot stood to one side, silent testimony to the valet's nightly vigil over his noble—and dying—master. The table, littered with bottles and vials of medicines, spoke of the attempts to stave off the inevitable. Somewhat disturbed by these unmistakable signs of illness, Ashtead opened the connecting door and stepped into the bedchamber beyond.

The room had been furnished for comfort and elegance, with the former predominating. Overstuffed chairs, red velvet hangings, cluttered occasional tables, and silver candelabra met Ashtead's rapid, appraising glance. A fire crackled in the hearth, making the apartment insufferably warm. Perhaps the wizened figure lying immobile beneath the coverlet on the great canopied bed needed it that way.

As Ashtead approached, the parchmentlike face turned on the crisp linen pillowcase, and almost transparent lids opened to reveal eyes as hard and alert as they had been in his distant youth. The dry lips parted. "So, you decided to show your face at last," snapped Sylvester Valerius Reginald Langston, sixth Marquis of Shoreham. "Where have you been? Sent for you a week ago. What's the idea keeping me waiting?"

A smile tugged at Ashtead's mouth. "I am sorry, sir. I'd gone out of town for a few days. I only received your message the day before yesterday."

The old man glared at him. "Lucky for you, you came when you did. Another couple of days, and there'd have been nothing for you to do but crow over my remains."

"Hardly that, sir. I fully expect you to rally." It cost him an effort to keep an amused, acerbic note in his voice. The sight of his powerful, autocratic great-uncle reduced to this mere shell left him shaken.

"See—" began the marquis, but the sound turned into a rattling cough. "See if I don't," he continued when he could speak again. "Just to spite you all. What's it been, boy? Five years?"

"At least." Ashtead stared down at him. "As I remember, you told me never to show my face here until you'd been put to bed with a shovel."

A crackling laugh, as dry as paper, shook the marquis's frail shoulders. "Damme if I don't see all of you into the grave. Sit down, boy, sit down." He waved Ashtead toward one of the chairs with a feeble gesture of one age-spotted hand. "Called you here because I want to see my affairs settled before I die."

"What?" Ashtead ensconced himself as far from the hearth as he could manage. "Making another will? Am I to be cut out again?"

"No more than you'd deserve. You certainly haven't been trying to endear yourself to anyone of late."

Ashtead's eyes narrowed. "Coming from one of your reputation, that sounds a little odd, sir."

A rumble of summer thunder punctuated his comment, and a light spattering of rain tapped against the window pane. The storm, which had hovered heavy in the air for the last two days, seemed about to break at last.

"My reputation, my young buck, was not lost in gaming hells or by offending society with my lightskirts. No, hold your tongue, boy. I'm not saying I didn't know my share of the muslin company, but I didn't flaunt them in the face of society. You might strive for a little discretion."

Ashtead examined his carefully pared nails. "I've had my reasons."

"Discouraging a few matchmaking mammas on the catch for a title and fortune for their daughters." The old man nodded. "Better ways to do that, boy. Take it from an old hand. Merely sets up people's backs, going your way around."

Ashtead's jaw tightened. "I believe—"

His great-uncle cut him off with an imperious wave of his frail hand. "I heard that little piece you had on your arm at Vauxhall last week was a regular dasher."

"Oh, a diamond of the first water, sir. Do you doubt my taste?" His lip curled in a sneer, for no more than any gentleman did he like his movements reported on to his great-uncle. "And where, may I ask, do you get your information?" But he thought he could guess: Ponderby, that incurable old gossip, always anxious to spread the latest *on dits*—and preferably the crim. con. tales.

"I have my ways. I'm not quite cut off from the world yet, so don't think I don't know what's being said about you. I'll not have my name dragged through the mud. It's high time you settled down respectably." The old gentleman regarded him through half-closed lids. "You're the last of my name, and I've no desire to see it die out. Which brings me to why I wanted to see you."

Amusement, which had faded during the preceding exchange, resurfaced. "Ah, yes. The will. Tell me, sir, how have you changed it this time? Am I to be disinherited if I don't marry?"

The marquis glared at him. "I'm going to see my granddaughter properly provided for before I die."

"Edwina? Do you mean she isn't already? Lord, the chit must be what, one-and-twenty? Thought she'd be married off with a brood of her own by now." He considered a moment. "She was not here at dinner."

"She dined with me." The old man plucked at the coverlets, scowling.

Leaving *him,* Ashtead reflected, to the uninspiring company of his great-uncle's estate agent Mr. Bentley, his solicitor Mr. Joffrey, and the Reverend Mr. Crawley. What precisely that latter gentleman did here, Ashtead could not hazard a guess. The marquis had shunned the services of the Church during his life; it seemed unlikely he sought spiritual solace now. "Come to think about it," he added, frowning at the marquis, "I don't remember ever seeing her in town."

"She hasn't been. Kept her with me. Haven't wanted her courted by a pack of fortune hunters."

Ashtead straightened. "Good God, do you mean

you've kept the poor girl kicking her heels about this great barrack of yours? I should think she must have gone mad with boredom by now."

"Not she. She belongs here." A note of pride sounded in the old gentleman's voice. "Knows the lands, knows the people. Always busy." He glanced at Ashtead, then looked away. "Thing is, she's never had a Season, never met any marriageable gentlemen."

Ashtead frowned. "Do you want me to have my sister present her? Lydia is just out of mourning for her husband. She could bring Edwina out in the Little Season—"

"I want you to marry her!" snapped Shoreham.

"You—" Ashtead stared at him in disbelief.

"Keep your tongue!" ordered the marquis. "She's a good girl, but like as not if I turned her loose on the town, she'd pick some unsuitable upstart. Chits take romantic notions into their heads. Don't want her made miserable by some young jackanapes."

"And what makes you think she'd be happy with me?" demanded Ashtead.

The marquis made a sound that in his younger and stronger days would have been a derisive snort. "Because you're like me. Too much so. Why, we could never get along for more than five minutes at a time. She'll know how to deal with your starts and tempers."

"Thank you. And she has already agreed to this?"

The marquis waved that aside. "She'll do as she's bid."

Ashtead drew an enameled snuff box from his pocket. "Crushed all the spirit out of her, have you?" He opened the box with a practiced flick of his thumb.

A choke of a laugh escaped the marquis. "No need. You'll find her lively enough. But she hasn't any more choice in the matter than you have."

Ashtead stopped in the act of reaching for a pinch. "There you are mistaken. Whatever has put the daft notion into your head that I would agree to this nonsense?"

"Oh, you'll agree. She'll suit you a damned sight better than those high fliers of yours. Bred to be lady of the manor. Knows her station. She'll fill the position, never you fear."

"Well," said Ashtead candidly, "she won't, because I won't have her."

A smug smile tugged at the thin mouth. "You'll marry her, all right."

"That, sir, is where you are wrong. When I marry, it will be when I choose and to whom I choose."

The smile thinned. "You'll choose."

A touch of ice crept into Ashtead's voice. "I'm no puppet to dance to your piping."

"Are you not?"

Ashtead stood abruptly, his ready temper threatening to overcome him. "I can only assume you are joking, sir. But I fail to find this in the least amusing."

"No reason for you to." The marquis waved toward the chair. "Sit down. This arguing is tiring me. You will marry the chit, so let us have no more nonsense about it."

Cold fury, so common in his dealings with his autocratic relative, surged through Ashtead. "Be damned if I will. There is nothing that can make me marry her or anyone else! And if that's the only reason you called me down here, I'll take my leave of you. We have nothing further to say to one another." He gave his great-uncle a curt nod and strode toward the door.

"High histrionics, my boy," came the shaky voice in much the tone of one playing his hidden ace, "but you are forgetting my will."

Ashtead turned around very slowly. Outside the window, a ragged streak of lightning brightened the storm-darkened sky. Thunder crashed only moments later, and the glass pane rattled with the rising wind. When the noise subsided, Ashtead said with slow deliberation, "Damn you, sir, and damn your will."

"Hah!" A choking cough set his great-uncle's shoulders shaking. "Did you pay attention this afternoon when Bentley showed you the books?"

Ashtead folded his arms before him. "Enough so I know which properties are entailed."

"And are you aware that the ones that are *not* are the ones that bring in the income?"

Ashtead's brows snapped down. "What the devil do you mean?"

"What I mean," Shoreham enunciated with care, "is that I can't stop you from inheriting my title or the castle or the Ashtead properties you already hold. I *can* however, stop you from inheriting the monies you'll need to run it all. That came to me through my wife's family. Nothing to do with your father."

Ashtead allowed his lip to curl. "You'd have me believe you'd allow your estates, your charities, to fall apart for lack of funds after your death? That's doing it too brown, sir."

"They won't fall apart, because you won't let them. You'll do whatever you have to for the good of your lands, and you know it. It's all well and good to tell me to go to the devil—I probably shall, very shortly—but remember, I know how you handle your lands. I gave you the Ashtead estates when you came of age, and Bentley has kept me informed of your doings. You may be a rake and a profligate, but he says you're a good landlord. I'll put a stop to the former by making use of the latter." He sank back against the pillows, his eyes closing. "You'll marry my granddaughter, settle down, and take care of my holdings."

"With the money you leave to her." A sneer colored Ashtead's words.

The old fingers clenched on the coverlet. "I am leaving her nothing. If you do not marry her before I die, every last bit of unentailed properties and monies will go to charity, and she will be penniless."

A stab of unease shot through him, but he forced confidence into his voice. "You wouldn't do that to your own granddaughter."

The old man looked up, his expression grim. "Wouldn't I? But it won't come to that. She'll marry you. Damn it, boy, I'm going to see you settled. You've been a dashed sight too rackety by half these last few years. I probably should have brought you here to learn the management of all my concerns, but we've never been able to be together more than ten minutes without falling out. Well, I've made my mistakes, and there's no undoing them now. Have to make the best of a bad business."

"Meaning me?" Ashtead said. "If you think so highly of me, I'm surprised you'd inflict me on your poor Edwina."

"You'll do. Nothing wrong with you the right female can't set straight."

Ashtead's eyes narrowed. "That's what that damned parson's doing here!"

The marquis nodded. "Thought of everything. Got the special license and the parson, and my solicitor to remake the will once the knot is tied. I can still drive a difficult team to an inch, my boy, and don't you forget it."

Ashtead gave a short, furious laugh. "You're ditched. I'll have none of your devil's bargain. I'll deal with the lands as best I can, and Edwina may look out for herself."

He turned on his heel and strode from the room, down the long corridor, accompanied by the rumbling thunder and the slashing of rain on the window behind him. He'd leave the Castle at once. Order his man to pack, have his curricle brought round, be out of here within the half hour. And then his great-uncle, his parson, his solicitor, and Edwina might all be damned, and with his blessings.

He reached his chamber, yanked on the bell rope, then strode to the window to glare out. The sooner he left this rattling old ruin behind . . . Another flash of lightning gave him pause. Damn the old gentleman for picking such a night. He couldn't take his horses out in this. He'd just have to wait until it cleared. Summer storms usually wore out their violence within a few hours. He'd be gone before morning.

The slight middle-aged figure of Ottley, that superior gentleman's gentleman who had served him for the past eleven years, entered the room with a silence and dignity designed not to intrude on his master's notorious humors. Ashtead glanced over his shoulder at him. "Brandy," he said. "A very great deal of it."

Ottley's expression remained impassive. "Very good, m'lord."

"And when you have brought it," Ashtead went on, the savagery still in his voice, "you may pack our things. We are leaving the instant this clears."

A flicker of concern showed in Ottley's eyes, but experience taught wisdom, and he said nothing. He departed, only to return a very few minutes later with a full decanter and a glass. These he set on a table, then turned to the cupboard where, only a few hours before, he had bestowed the contents of his master's valises.

Ashtead splashed the alcohol into the glass and threw himself into the chair that stood before the hearth. Anger still raged within him, at his grandfather for trying to manage his life in so outrageous a fashion, at himself for having come here at all, at Edwina just for existing. At the storm, for preventing his immediate departure. He glared out at the sky that darkened into night, and swore.

"Very aptly phrased, m'lord," said his highly privileged valet from the depths of the cupboard.

"Oh, to the devil with you too," snapped Ashtead.

"Very probably, m'lord," came the unruffled response. "Especially as you seem wishful to speed matters along by leaving this night."

Ashtead glared at him, then turned his attention to the contents of the glass he held. Recklessly, he tossed it off; the smooth liquid sent fire shooting down his throat. He poured another, swallowed half the contents in one gulp, then became aware of the irritating nature of the sounds of Ottley opening drawers and shaking out linens. Still glowering into the hearth, he ordered, "Leave it for now, man. Get out."

"Certainly, m'lord." His man eyed him with tolerant resignation. "I suppose you would wish me to bring you another decanter?"

Ashtead glared at the rain that pelted the window with determined force. "You might as well."

The door opened and closed again behind his valet, and Ashtead returned to his contemplation of his folly in ever having answered his great-uncle's summons in the first place. What the devil was the man about, trying to foist an unwanted wife onto him? Well, he was every bit as stubborn and strong-willed as the old man. He would not cave in.

And Edwina and her future were not his problems. Once the old gentleman saw he was serious in his refusal, he would break down and provide for the girl. Except, Ashtead reflected with a sudden ruefulness, the old gentleman was every bit as stubborn and strong-willed as was he. Once the marquis had sworn his word to something, he would not go back on it. Edwina would indeed be left penniless. But that was no reason he should be forced into marrying her.

He noticed he'd emptied his second glass and poured a third. He could get along without his great-uncle's fortune. Somehow, he'd find a way to manage the estates. He could turn them around, make them more profitable. And as for the charitable concerns . . . He considered, absently finishing his glass and pouring another. He'd be forced to close the orphanages. Lord, how many children would be left without a home, without food, because he wouldn't bow to his great-uncle's high-handed tactics? How many tenants and servants and farm workers would find themselves out of jobs and places to live? The contents of the decanter lowered again, then again.

The entailed properties were not profitable, he'd seen that in the books. And if there had been any way of making them carry their weight, his great-uncle and Bentley would have found it. He reached for the decanter and missed. On the third try, he succeeded in splashing the liquid on the table at his side before his aim settled on the glass. He swallowed the contents before any of it could escape.

None of this would be his fault. The marquis had it in his power to assure the well-being of everyone and everything. He was just too stubborn, too determined to have the driving of Ashtead, too set on having his own way. And all those people would suffer because of it.

Ashtead would suffer too, knowing he could have prevented their hardship, knowing he could have secured the funds to keep all running as it should.

Once his great-uncle was dead, *he* would be the Marquis of Shoreham. All these people would look to him. He had to be able to help them.

He drained the last of the decanter into his glass and set it back on the table, only to have it roll sideways, over the edge, to crash with a splintering of crystal onto the Aubusson carpet. He stared at it, bemused, his mind fuddled with drink. It was like his life, fragmented by a moment's occurrence. With a shaking hand, he raised his glass, saluted the ruins on the floor, and swallowed the last of the brandy.

Only one solution to the dilemma presented itself. Only his total capitulation. It was inevitable, and he knew it. He couldn't harm so many people.

Rage, temporarily lulled by drink, surged through him once more. With an effort, he dragged himself erect, staggered a few steps, and collapsed against a bedpost, clutching it to keep his feet. No choice. Damn the old gentleman. No choice. The refrain repeated over and over in his mind. No choice, damn him, no choice. He thrust himself free of his support and made it as far as the door, where he clung to the handle, steadying himself. His head spun; impotent fury and a full decanter of brandy proved a powerful, driving force.

Somehow he made it into the corridor, where he propped himself against a wall. No, against a painting. He blinked at the Roman-nosed dowager from the time of Queen Anne who glared down at him, unseeing and uncaring. He swept her an unsteady bow, made his apologies, and resumed his wavering progress toward his great-uncle's chamber.

He didn't knock this time. He simply opened the door and staggered in, spinning head held high, determined that if he must martyr himself, he would do it with dignity. He blinked bleary eyes; candlelight filled the chamber, and some female, a lanky, dowdy miss, stood at the bedside. His great-uncle now sat up against his pillows, clutching a number of cards. Others lay scattered across the blanket in a haphazard fashion, as if cast down with some force.

Ashtead drew himself to his full height and swayed. "Very well, damn you," he enunciated with care. "Bring on your parson. If I must go through with this marriage, it had best be now, while I'm three parts disguised. I'll never go through with it sober." Somehow, the speech hadn't quite come out the way he'd planned. He slammed one fist into his other palm. It seemed a good, dramatic gesture.

The marquis had grown unaccountably fuzzy. For that matter, the whole room had grown fuzzy. It spun about him, walls and ceilings and carpeted floors changing places with dizzying speed. He took a step forward, everything kilted at strange angles, and a welcome, muffling darkness wrapped about him.

Lady Edwina Langston gazed down at the crumpled figure of the viscount where he sprawled, unconscious, on the carpet, and her lip curled in distaste. She made no move to go to his aid; the servants were welcome to clean up this mess, as far as she was concerned. Instead, she turned the penetrating gaze of her large gray eyes on her grandfather. "This is the fine husband you have chosen for me? You honor me, sir."

"Oh, be still, girl," came the irritated old voice. "He's just playing off a fit of temper at being outmaneuvered. He'll do, once he's sober."

"I see. How delightful. I have always dreamt of a bridegroom who must drink himself into a stupor in order to bring himself to the point of offering for me."

"Don't be missish, girl!" snapped the old gentleman.

"I'm not in the least. I merely marveled at the rare compliment the pair of you have made me."

His watery eyes narrowed. "What's the matter, afraid you're not up to the task of handling him?"

She eyed him with a smoldering anger. "Not in the least. I merely have no intention of trying."

"Enough of this." He waved a peevish hand. "I'm growing tired. Send Stebbings to me and go to bed. You may marry Ashtead in the morning."

"No." She had to force the calmness into her voice. "I will not." She waited a moment, her defiance bristling, but he made no further comment. He sank back against the pillows, his eyes closing, the cards slipping from his slackened grip. He might be asleep, or he might be pretending in order to stem her defiance. Either way, it made little difference; she would gain nothing further by remaining. "And you may summon your valet yourself," she informed him, and turned on her heel.

She might have had more confidence in the effect of her exit if she could feel certain he had seen it. But she could not. She let herself through to the antechamber, where she discovered the elderly valet beside the medicine table, mixing his master's cordial. Stebbings looked up at her, his expression worried. "You may go to him," she snapped. "And Lord Ashtead will require conveyance to his chamber."

She swept out of the room, carried by the temper she had kept in check out of long years of deference to her grandfather. He had made unreasonable demands of her before, such as keeping her at his side instead of requesting one of their distant relations to launch her into society. He had kept her a virtual prisoner here, preventing any chance of her meeting anyone. And had it all been for this? To force her into marriage with that ramshackle, drunken rakehell?

She blinked to clear the mist that filled her eyes, that threatened to spill down her cheeks. Did he truly think she would be flattered to be prized so highly? She had borne much over the.years, because she had no choice. But this utter lack of concern for her feelings, for her sensibilities, for her future, proved too much; she could stand no more. She would escape, now, before her grandfather could have her stopped. She would pack a valise and leave the Castle, leave behind the autocratic old man and her insulting bridegroom.

She stormed into her apartment, glanced about, then dragged open her wardrobe. She'd take a morning gown, and a fresh chemise, and her night rail, and a comb and brush. She tossed items onto the bed at random, grasping the first articles of clothing she encountered. Lacking so much as a bandbox, she bundled her few chosen items into a shawl and knotted it into a sling to hang over her shoulder. She thrust her feet into half-boots of kid leather, dragged on a cloak, and tossed the hood over her sleeked back hair. Then, grabbing up her bundle, she let herself out of her chamber.

The gas lamps offered a pale light on the great curving staircase. She ran down carpeted oak steps, wanting only to escape, to distance herself from this abominable household. Her footsteps echoed across the marble-tiled hall, but she refused to let that trouble her. Just let anyone try to stop her, she fumed as she dragged the bolt back from the front door with a wrenching screech that would have brought anyone within hearing at the run. But no one would be that close; the servants all would be about their own affairs, preparing for their beds and their early rising the following morning.

The drizzling rain startled her, and she looked up into the sky, remembering for the first time the torrential downpour of earlier in the evening. A distant rumble of thunder announced the storm had moved on. Well, getting a little wet would be a small price to pay for her escape. She dragged the door closed behind her with a slam and set forth down the steps and along the drive.

Outraged hurt and anger carried her forward. How dared her grandfather decree she must marry the vile Ashtead? She knew his reputation, the reason her grandfather had barred his doors to his heir. The servants had discussed it with relish prior to his arrival; she had the word of her maid for that. Though how any poor, misguided female could fall under his spell—

She thrust aside a sudden memory of her own impression of him as she had peeped from behind the draperies in the Gold Salon to watch his arrival. She hadn't known her grandfather's intentions then, had looked merely with the eyes of curiosity, and had had her breath swept away. But first impressions, she reassured herself, had little to do with reality. His actions had revealed his true nature, and all too clearly. Well, she was no milk-and-water miss to bow submissively to anyone's decrees, and so Ashtead and her grandfather would shortly discover.

Her rage carried her past the garden of the gatehouse, through the gap in the hedge, and onto the country lane. Her toes squelched within her boots, testimony to the numerous puddles she had failed to avoid. Only the faintest light illumined the night; heavy clouds obscured the moon and stars. But she was no faintheart to let such a minor matter bother her, not when she had struck so bold a blow to gain her freedom.

That triumphant thought carried her another half mile and through several more muddy puddles. During the next quarter mile, it dawned on her she had no idea where she went. Nor had she included any money among the few items she had packed. Why should she have? She had never needed it before, for on her rare expeditions from the Castle, she had been hedged about with servants who tended to all the details. It occurred to her that she might very well need money now, and possibly a great deal of it. Her steps slowed, but she kept doggedly on. She would not, *could* not, go back.

Which meant she had to go *somewhere*.

At the moment, the only place of which she could think was the crossroads, three miles farther on. She did her best to postpone thinking about her plight, but every step became harder to take, the continuing drizzle adding to the lowness of her spirits as her anger faded, to be replaced by a growing apprehension that threatened to turn into fear. By the time she reached the posting road, with its milestone marker and cross-arms indicating directions, weariness had overtaken her and she could do no more than sink down on the low stone post.

She was a fool, she knew that, but a fool with some measure of pride. It would not allow her to return to her grandfather's home, where she'd never been valued, only been treated as an unpaid companion to the high-handed old gentleman. And now he regarded her as nothing more than a commodity. She could not bear to have her life ordered by men who cared nothing for her.

But she could not sit here in the rain forever.

She looked up into the night sky, and the chill misty drizzle drenched her face. It had cleared somewhat; she could make out individual clouds, and a silvery glow that told her where the moon rode high in the sky. The shadowy shapes drifted, and one star peeped out, then another, then a third. The moon struggled out from behind its shield, and a soft radiance flooded down on her. A full moon.

Emptiness rushed through her, followed by fear, and a deep, all-encompassing longing. What, she wondered suddenly, would she wish for if she could ask for anything, anything at all? Freedom? Security? She considered, then her heart filled with one desire, to never again be dependent on anyone else. She put every ounce of her being into that wish as she gazed at the creamy moon with the wispy gray clouds floating before it.

But what good was a wish? None in the least, she told herself. She sat on her milepost, cold, wet, and wretched, hugging herself, sure of only one thing: Whatever else might become of her, she could never return to her grandfather's home.

A spark flashed before her, glowing brilliant yellow before it extinguished. Then a green one flashed, followed in rapid succession by ones of violet, pink, blue, then all the colors at once. Roses began to rain down on her, intermingled with daisies, pinks, daffodils, pansies, poppies, and forget-me-nots. Butterflies, brilliant oranges and blues, yellows and greens, darted among them in glorious confusion. And everywhere in the air fluttered tiny fairies playing miniature violins, flutes, oboes, and horns. Their lively, tinkling melody filled the air.

In their midst appeared a Liny figure, human except for the double set of oval fairy wings. The figure grew larger, a middle-aged woman with long fair hair plaited into braids that hung in ropes about her head, fastened in place by tiny violets. Laughing eyes, full of mischief, smiled at Edwina. The woman stepped forward onto the carpet of flowers, shaking butterflies from her shimmering silver tunic.

"Go on, shoo!" The woman sent a few reluctant butterflies on their way with a wave of her hand. A solitary rounded feather drifted down to join the colorful pile of petals. She tilted her head to one side and regarded Edwina through the flowers that continued to drift to the ground. "I have come in answer to your wish, my love."

Edwina opened her mouth, then closed it again, shaking her head in utter bewilderment.

A merry laugh escaped the little woman. "Do you not want an opportunity to become independent?"

"Yes, but—" Edwina broke off, the longing returning to fill her heart, vying with her confusion.

"Then let us settle the details." The woman hummed a lively air, and the flowers shot into the air to form a canopy. A table appeared, laid with cups and plates, a pot of tea, and a plate heaped with biscuits and cakes. "We might as well be comfortable," the woman said, and beamed at her. "I am Xanthe, your fairy godmother. And this"—she gestured to an immense white cat who leaped to the table to sniff the cream pitcher—"is Titus. And you," she added, her eyes brimming with merriment, "are about to embark on the most delightful adventure."

Two

Edwina stood at the window of the sunny breakfast parlor, gazing across the Marine Parade, across the expanse of rippled sand to the bathing machines and the children at play beside the ocean. Brighton. She couldn't quite believe it, couldn't believe the change in her circumstances, couldn't believe she had been rescued from the disaster of her heedless flight for freedom.

A fairy godmother?

If she weren't here, she wouldn't believe it. It still didn't seem possible. One moment she'd been sitting in the chill, wet night, ready to burst into tears at the hopelessness of her position, and the next everything had changed, like magic.

She smiled at that phrase. Exactly like magic. She'd been treated to a much-needed tea—with a touch of brandy to ward off the ill effects of the drenching she'd endured. Then she'd been seated warm and snug and dry, surrounded by the sensation of laughter, of someone caring about her, in a traveling chariot that had appeared out of nowhere. No, out of the flowers that had been strewn about the ground. And the carriage had been pulled by butterflies.

And now here she was, in Brighton for the summer season. Eight weeks, in which she had the opportunity to find a way in which to ensure she would never again be dependent on anyone.

Only how she was to do that, she had no idea.

Titus leaped to the windowsill and fixed her with a stare of feline intensity. Very slowly, the green eyes closed, then opened again.

Edwina stroked the long, soft fur. "How does one become independent?" she asked the immense animal.

He merely blinked again and deigned to rub his head against her hand.

"Did you sleep well?" asked a light, merry voice from the doorway.

Edwina turned to see her fairy godmother entering the room. Gone was the flowing tunic of the night before. She now wore a fashionable flounced morning gown of a vastly becoming shade of light blue, a strand of pearls, and a confection of lace, ribands, and flowers perched on her wayward braids. Gone too were the disconcerting wings. But never would Xanthe seem ordinary.

"Sleep?" the fairy repeated, her eyes dancing with laughter.

"Oh. Yes. Amazingly well," Edwina managed.

The fairy beamed, and it dawned on Eddie that her deep, restful slumbers just might have had supernatural help. On the whole, she decided she was grateful for the gift of reviving repose. She'd been confused, frightened, aghast at her own recklessness. Now— Well, she was still confused, frightened, and aghast at her own recklessness. But at least she was no longer so tired she couldn't face it.

Xanthe inspected the contents of a chafing dish, nodded in approval, and filled a plate with eggs, sweet-smelling buns, and wafers of something that Eddie suspected was not really meat, though the delicious aromas emanating from the pot told her otherwise. She filled her own plate, added a few wafers of the not-quite-meat to slip to Titus, then took her place at the table. "I don't think I took it all in last night," Eddie said.

"No." Xanthe's amusement threatened to bubble over. "But it is really quite simple. I have granted you the opportunity to never again be dependent upon anyone. You will stay here with me for the next eight weeks—"

"Yes, but how?" Eddie broke in. "That is what troubles me. How am I to achieve independence? Unless you . . ." Her voice trailed off as she regarded the fairy with uncertainty.

Xanthe shook her head, a touch regretfully. "As I told you last night, I may only grant opportunities, not solutions. Those are entirely up to you."

"But what am I to do?" Eddie shook her head, her sense of hopelessness returning. "I have no more than a couple hundred pounds from my mamma, and my grandfather will cut me off utterly for running away like this."

"Do you really think so?" The gentle, amused eyes watched her.

Eddie considered, then nodded. "He has never been able to brook any form of opposition. I had an aunt, you must know, though I never met her. She died some years ago. When she was seventeen, Grandfather chose a husband for her, but she had fallen in love with another. Quite a respectable gentleman, Pappa said. The heir to a barony, not some fortune hunter or anyone unacceptable. But Grandfather forbade the banns, of course. So rather than wed his choice, my aunt fled to Gretna with her young gentleman, and Grandfather forbade anyone to ever mention her name to him again." She looked up, troubled. "So you see, he will not have the slightest hesitation in casting me off as well."

"Are you regretting running away?"

Eddie considered, then slowly, surprised, shook her head. "I might well be if you hadn't appeared," she admitted. "But in daylight, with the storm past, and surrounded by such luxury—" She waved a hand, indicating the elegantly appointed apartment, then shook her head. "It gives me hope."

Xanthe nodded, pleased, and took a bite of her cinnamon-laced roll. "Hope is half the battle," she assured Eddie. "It opens you to possibilities, while despair permits you to see nothing but failure."

"It is hard to envision success," Eddie admitted. Though here, in the comfort of this shelter—this temporary shelter, she reminded herself—her situation seemed less hopeless. "The problem," she went on at last, "is *how* to become independent. Normally one inherits money, or is awarded a small competence by a relative. I will have been cut out of Grandfather's will, and as for my only other relative, my mamma's brother, he is far more likely to come to *me* for help."

Xanthe nodded. "Mr. Marmaduke Rutland. A very entertaining gentleman, though sorely improvident."

Eddie brightened. "Do you know him?"

The fairy's mischievous smile flashed. "I know everyone it is useful for me to know, my love."

Eddie sighed. "How easy everything must be when you are a fairy godmother."

"It helps," Xanthe agreed. "But magic never solves problems. Remember that, my love. You must reach within yourself to find the real answers."

Eddie gave an exaggerated sigh. "I was afraid it wouldn't be as easy as I hoped. Well," she said, returning to the matter that troubled her mind, "since there is no one to give me what I need, I must find it for myself. Somehow."

"And what is it precisely you want?" The smile lingered in the fairy's eyes.

Eddie had started to lift her teacup, but she stopped, staring at Xanthe.

"You have never considered," Xanthe pointed out.

Slowly, Eddie lowered the cup to its saucer. "No, I have not. Oh, I've dreamed of escaping, of going to London, of having a Season, but I've never gotten beyond that, to what would happen next."

"Do you wish to marry?" prompted the fairy.

"No!" Her own vehemence surprised Eddie. "No," she continued, more calmly. "I thought once, when I was quite young and filled with romantic notions, how wonderful it would be to have some knight all dressed in shining armor to storm the Castle and whisk me away. But would it be much different living with him than living with my grandfather? I have the most horrid fear he would make all the decisions and tell me what I must or must not do, and hedge me about with the most stifling restrictions, and I could not *bear* that."

"You want to be independent," Xanthe agreed.

"Yes!" A shaky sigh tore from Eddie. "I want to make my own decisions. I don't ever want to have anyone deciding my life for me again."

Xanthe nodded. "Excellent. That's the first step. Now you must consider where, and in what manner, you would like to live. One must have clear pictures in one's mind before the appropriate actions can be taken to obtain those ends."

Eddie sipped her tea. Part of her mind noted it remained as hot as when she had first poured it. It also seemed to have refilled itself, to the same strength and sweetness as before. "I have always lived quietly," she said at last. "I believe I should like to go on doing so. That will be the most practical, at least. I shouldn't need much money if I were to purchase a tiny cottage in a village somewhere. Just a small income to cover the necessary expenses."

Xanthe nodded again. "We are making progress. Now, we must consider how you are to obtain this."

Eddie sighed. "That is where my plan falls apart," she admitted. "I am wholly lacking in any talent that might earn me any sort of a competence."

"How much do you think you would need?" Xanthe inquired.

Eddie drew a deep breath, which brought the scent of cinnamon buns to her. She spotted a platter of them before her, selected one, and took a mouth-watering bite. "I am not certain," she said slowly when she could speak again, "but I should think ten thousand pounds, safely invested in the Funds, should do it. But I might as well wish for the moon. How am I to obtain such a sum? That's a fortune!"

"Only to some," pointed out Xanthe. "To others, it's a mere drop in a bucket."

"Like my grandfather." Eddie took another sip of tea. "Only, he inherited some and married the rest. I must discover how to earn it." Moodily, she bit into the roll again. "I cannot paint or write," she went on when she had swallowed. "I cannot sing, I am hopeless at charades, so I would never be able to tread the boards. I can sew a creditable hem, but my attempts to design my own dresses have failed utterly, so I cannot set myself up as a *modiste*. Nor a milliner," she added, memories of her attempts to decorate a bonnet inflicting themselves on her mind. "The only occupations available to a female would be as dreary as they would be unlucrative. It would take me several lifetimes to save that much on a governess's salary, and I cannot think of any poor soul more ordered about than a governess, unless it is a companion."

Titus settled in the chair at her side, his massive tail wrapping about his feet. He fixed her with the plaintive regard of a cat who has not eaten in days. She handed him one of the pieces of not-quite-meat, which he sniffed, then deigned to accept.

Xanthe's eyes glittered. "You spoke of your Uncle Marmaduke."

A sudden smile warmed Eddie. "Dear Uncle Marmaduke. How long it has been. But he is quite hopeless, you must know. He's a gamester, and is forever under the hatches. I don't know how many times he applied to Pappa to save him from a sponging house. He is probably languishing in one now," she added, her smile fading. "Grandfather forbade him entry to the Castle when Mamma and Pappa died, and I have not heard from him since."

"Is he a clever gamester?" Xanthe asked.

A reminiscent smile tugged at her lips. "Not as much as he needs to be, I fear. He taught me his tricks during one of his last visits, and unless he has improved since then, even I could defeat him now. Piquet is Grandfather's one passion," she explained. "I have played it with him every night for so long, it feels as if I have never done anything else with—" She broke off, staring at Xanthe. "Oh, the notion is absurd."

"Is it?" The fairy's eyes twinkled.

"If only I could play for more than chicken stakes,"

Eddie said, finishing her thought, "I believe I might soon have my competence."

Xanthe hummed a soft bar of music, and the coffeepot rose from the sideboard, sailed across the table, and hovered over the fairy's cup, refilling it. "It would not need to be *much* more than chicken stakes, would it?"

Eddie stared at her. "You're not seriously suggesting—"

A dimple formed in Xanthe's cheek. "You would not need to win it all in one night," she pointed out. "Our agreement is that you may stay in Brighton with me for eight weeks. And since this is the summer season—"

"—there are any number of fashionables staying here who might welcome an evening of play to relieve their boredom," Eddie finished, musing. "But we cannot possibly set ourselves up as a gaming establishment!"

"No, indeed not!" Xanthe laughed. "You would not wish to gain such a reputation."

"No!" Eddie agreed. "It would be quite shocking."

"But cards are played at every ball, and in every home, as part of every entertainment."

Eddie stared at her fairy godmother, her mind beginning to race. Ten thousand pounds would be an incredible amount for a lady to win. But if she didn't think of it as a single, lump sum, if she saw it instead in increments—

Ten sets of one thousand pounds each. No, even that was too much, would attract unwelcome comment. What of twenty sets—twenty nights—of five hundred pounds? That was more reasonable. Or better, thirty nights of what, about three hundred and fifty pounds each? That might be possible. A lady could win that without evoking scandalized comment. And she had eight weeks.

About fifty-six nights. That would allow for evenings she could not play, for the times she won only a little.

And she would win. She had no doubts about that at all. She knew the game in all its subtleties, had mastered it long ago playing against her father, her uncle, her grandfather, their friends, all of whom had taught her tricks and strategies, never realizing the great gift they bestowed upon her. She could win. She could achieve her independence. She could be free of her autocratic grandfather and the vile Ashtead. It was possible.

She looked up to find Xanthe watching her in amusement. "How does one set about beginning a career as a genteel gamestress?" Eddie asked.

Xanthe laughed. "By being invited somewhere, of course. Shall we stroll over to Donaldson's Lending Library this morning? I feel certain we shall encounter an old acquaintance who will be devastated if we do not attend her gathering this evening."

"Who?"

Xanthe shook her head, her mysterious smile playing about her lips. "How should I know? We haven't encountered her yet. But first we must do something about your appearance, my love."

Eddie cast a doubtful glance over her much-worn morning gown of sprigged muslin. "Is there anything amiss?"

"Quite out of fashion," Xanthe assured her. "And with your complexion, you should have something with a bit more color. Like this." The fairy hummed a bar of music. "What do you think?"

Eddie followed the direction of Xanthe's gaze, and stared down at a peach-colored muslin walking dress with a spencer of russet brown sarcenet. She sprang to her feet, alarmed by this unnoticed alteration in her garments.

"Do you not like it?" Xanthe hummed again, and the muslin and spencer changed to shades of green.

"How—" Eddie began, shaken.

A rippling laugh escaped Xanthe. "I am sorry, my love. I forget that magic can be somewhat startling when you're not used to it. In a day or two you'll hardly notice." She hummed softly, and the rolls on the plate transformed into a score of butterflies that fluttered together to form the outline of one large swallowtail.

"Now," Xanthe went on. "Did you prefer the peach, or would you perhaps like rose or blue?" Another hummed bar brought about the different colors.

"The—the rose," Eddie managed.

The butterflies, apparently forgotten by Xanthe, drifted to the flower arrangement before the window. Eddie looked from them to her gown, then back again. She would actually grow accustomed to this? It didn't seem possible.

"A bonnet too, don't you think?" Xanthe added.

Eddie barely heard the haunting measure of music before she felt the weight on her head. She went to the mirror above the sideboard and inspected a high poke-straw bonnet, decorated with a cluster of ribands in shades to match both gown and spencer. And when had her hair become all ringlets and curls? She had dressed it this morning as usual, smoothed back into a chignon. But Xanthe had worked her magic there as well, with the result that Eddie barely recognized the modish image that stared back at her.

"Let us go show you off," Xanthe declared. But instead of leading the way to the front door, Xanthe took her to the salon, a spacious room decorated in the first style of elegance in tones of ivory, blue, and gold. The butterflies accompanied them, as did Titus, who leapt lightly to the window ledge, where he sprawled in the sun.

Eddie watched, surprised, as the fairy settled in a comfortable chair. "I thought—"

"We are about to have a visitor, my love." Even as Xanthe spoke, a knock sounded from the street.

Eddie stared at her fairy godmother, amazed. "Do you know *everything?*" she demanded in awe.

Xanthe merely laughed and turned her expectant face to the door.

Footsteps sounded in the hall, and the panel opened to reveal a footman garbed in the blue and silver livery that Xanthe seemed to have adopted as her own. In a clear, carrying voice, the young man announced. "Lord Ashtead, my lady," and stepped aside to allow the visitor to enter.

Eddie drew an involuntary step backward, and the gaze of her widening eyes flew in frantic appeal to Xanthe. But her fairy godmother remained unruffled, regarding the new arrival with that mischievous smile playing about her mouth. Eddie's hand clenched the back of a chair, her knuckles whitening.

Ashtead strode in, tall, broad-shouldered, elegant in a coat of blue Bath cloth, fawn-colored pantaloons, and gleaming Hessians. The intricate folds of his impeccably starched neckcloth could have caused a dandy to swoon with envy, but there was nothing the least bit foppish about the viscount. His well-formed figure and tanned, rugged features bespoke the sportsman, and his assured manner bespoke a gentleman at home to a peg in the highest reaches of society. For one, treacherous moment, Eddie saw him again through her more innocent vision of the afternoon before, when he'd seemed to her the epitome of her daydreams.

But then his drunken, insulting, insufferable behavior had turned his presence into a nightmare.

Xanthe rose and glided forward, both hands extended. "I thought you would not be long, dear boy."

To Eddie's utter amazement, Ashtead grasped the fairy's hands, then bent forward to kiss her cheek.

Xanthe cast a glance filled with wicked amusement at her, then returned her attention to the viscount. "Did you have a pleasant journey?"

"Except for the inevitable worry that Lady Edwina might not have reached you safely." His gaze traveled to where Eddie stood behind the chair, framed against the window, and his brow creased into a puzzled frown.

Did he not recognize her, the lady he had agreed to marry? But he had not seen her upon his arrival at the Castle, as she had glimpsed him. In fact, they had not met in years; he probably retained no more than the vaguest memories of a hoydenish, half-grown schoolroom miss. The only time they had been together in the same room had been last night in her grandfather's chamber, and she could not remember him sparing so much as a glance at her during that brief minute before the drink had gotten the better of him.

Now, he more than made up for it. His steady gaze moved from the top of her bonnet to linger on her face, then moved down her figure to the toes of her slippers, which peeped out from beneath the ruffled flounce of her skirt. An expression of perplexity settled on his features. "Edwina?" he asked, his tone one of disbelief.

She inclined her head the merest fraction.

He rallied. "That was a fine stunt you pulled on us,

running out as you did. Your grandfather flew off in a high rage."

Her chin thrust out at his argumentative tone. "And I doubt he's any the worse for it. In fact, I fancy it did him a world of good."

"No." Ashtead still frowned. "He was in the devil of a taking. Couldn't think where you could have gone to until he remembered your godmother."

Eddie straightened her shoulders. "If he sent you after me to fetch me home, you may tell him, with my compliments, that I am remaining right where I am."

Ashtead drew an enameled snuff box from his pocket and flicked it open. "He didn't send me. He seemed more inclined to wash his hands of you." He helped himself to a pinch.

She stiffened. "Then why have you come?"

His smile, as sudden as it was unexpected, caused her breath to catch in her throat. How dare he affect her in such a way, when the mere thought of him repulsed her!

"I have come," he said with a touch of ruefulness, "to apologize for my unforgivable behavior of last night."

Her eyebrows rose. "Indeed?" She inserted as much coldness into the word as she could manage.

Something that might have been irritation flashed in his eyes. "I can only blame it on my abominable temper. My great-uncle always triggers it, and I, his. It is the reason I so rarely visit the Castle."

She sniffed. "I thought it was because he had ordered the servants to throw you out if you dared to show your face."

To her surprise, his lips twitched. She had expected that temper to flare at her, and had braced against its onslaught. Instead, she saw humor in his eyes.

"Precisely so. Though what he does to vent his spleen when I am not around, I can only wonder."

His smile was contagious, but she mastered the impulse to answer it. "He vents it upon anyone and everyone who comes near him."

His brow lowered. "Not on you surely."

"Not if I do as I am told, and play cards so that he always wins without being able to detect that I permit him to." She could not read his expression, and decided on the whole it might be better not to try. "It makes no matter," she added with an assumed airiness. "It need no longer concern me."

"But it can." He moved to the hearth, then turned, one hand resting on the mantel. "You may return to your home and have no fear I will allow myself to be coerced into offering for you again."

She raised her chin even further so she could look down her nose at him. "Does that mean you intend to abstain from drinking?" A dull flush crept across his cheekbones, and it pleased her to have scored a point.

He was silent a moment, then asked, "You are aware of how your grandfather is settling his affairs?"

She allowed her lip to curl. "He had the—the infinite kindness to tell me."

Ashtead nodded. "Precisely so. But I intend to return to the Castle and tell him he may do as he pleases with the unentailed properties, then leave. He should be sufficiently furious with me that if you go to him and make your apologies for your own fit of temper, he will probably leave everything to you, and most likely with the provision that you do *not* marry me."

Her mouth tightened. "Do you think I would go crawling back to him and beg his forgiveness? I am glad I left. In fact, I only wish I had done so earlier."

His brow lowered. "He has assured me you have no fortune of your own."

She hunched a shoulder. "I will accept nothing further from him."

He eyed her for a long moment. "You are still angry."

"And why should I not be?" she demanded. "He has treated me abominably, and as for you—" With considerable effort, she mastered her outburst. "I will not return," she repeated.

"Will your godmother—"

"I will take care of myself," she snapped quickly.

The furrows in his brow deepened. "You need not fear any further pressure because of me."

"As I have no intention of ever setting eyes upon you again, that seems quite likely."

"You won't," he snapped. "Once I have informed my great-uncle what he may do with himself and his fortune, I will not return to the Castle while he lives."

"You may do as you like, as long as you keep your distance from me."

His jaw clenched. "Rest assured, I have no desire whatsoever to marry you."

She awarded this sally a skeptical look.

His teeth ground audibly. "I will find another way to manage the estate and charitable concerns without his fortune."

"Oh, to be sure, that should pose no problems for you at all."

"You know perfectly well it will pose many problems," he shot back. "It won't be easy, and I admit I allowed Bentley to alarm me with the extent of the obligations that are tied to the title, but I will not fall prey to my great-uncle's machinations a second time." He drew a deep breath, then let it out. "Come, we have only to make it clear to him that we will neither of us agree to his preposterous suggestion, and you may be comfortable again."

"Or you might be." But she said the words under her breath, and he did not seem to hear. If she did as he suggested, returned home, she would be at the mercy of these two men once more. A penniless female had few options, and none of them good. She had her chance— thanks to Xanthe. She was not fool enough to throw it away, especially not at the urging of a man she had no reason to trust.

No matter how attractive he might be.

No sooner had the thought formed than she thrust it from her. She was not so foolish as to succumb to the charm he seemed able to turn on and off at will. And that he had come here to charm her—before she had set off his ready temper—she had not a doubt. He had certainly taken pains with his appearance, as if she might soften toward him after that unbearable slight of the previous night. She regarded him with open contempt. "Let us understand one another," she said, pronouncing each word with care. "I don't believe for a moment you intend to let my grandfather's fortune slip through your fingers. You may have every penny of it, for all I care. But understand this: You will never have me. And if marriage to me is indeed the only way you may win his money, then I am sorry for it, and for you." She pushed past him, not trusting herself to remain in the same room with him a moment longer.

And with luck, she would never have to see him again.

Three

Ashtead strode from the house and down the Marine Parade, seething. She had as good as called him a fortune hunter, and it made matters no better that she had cause. It didn't weigh in the least with her that he'd had to fly into the devil's own temper, and become as drunk as a wheelbarrow, before he'd been able to screw himself up to the pitch. In fact, odd creature that she was, it had seemed to annoy her even more. He considered that for a few minutes, decided there could be no understanding females in the least, and stalked down the street.

The fresh, salty tang of the sea air filled his lungs. From nearby came the screech of gulls circling over the shore where two fishermen had dragged a dory onto the sand. Several cats prowled, sniffing, searching for tidbits. He considered the tranquil scene, but it failed to lighten his mood.

Edwina had formed a damned low opinion of him. Well, what the devil did the chit want? He'd apologized, hadn't he? And now, away from his great-uncle's exacerbating manner, he had no intention of being goaded into offering for her again. Somehow, he'd contrive. Just how escaped him at the moment, but he'd do it.

He could count on Bentley to make suggestions, of course. Poor man, he'd feel the loss of fortune almost as strongly as Ashtead. He'd been the marquis's estate agent for the past seven-and-thirty years, and loved the place as if it were his own. If any way could be found to maintain the properties, Bentley would give his all to bring it about. And it did Ashtead no good whatsoever to wallow in guilt over allowing his temper—not to mention his finer feelings—to prevent him from securing the funds needed by the many obligations that accompanied the title and Castle.

He turned onto the Steyne, but had proceeded barely a dozen paces before he caught sight of an unmistakable figure, a lanky gentleman of medium height, gazing vacantly into space as he stood stock still, forcing pedestrians to maneuver around him. A slow, reluctant smile tugged at the corners of Ashtead's mouth, disturbing his ill humor. He hadn't seen Sir William Jacoby more than a half-dozen times in as many years, but it seemed his old friend from Eaton days hadn't changed in the least.

At the moment, Jacoby wore a disreputable coat, a simply knotted neckcloth, pantaloons that a more discriminating gentleman would have long ago cast away as a bad case, and Hessians that had not recently seen a brush or polishing cloth. Only the artless disorder of his fair curls bore a fashionable stamp, but as this was their natural state, Ashtead didn't fall into the error of believing his friend had squandered any time on their arrangement.

From long-remembered habit, Ashtead took Jacoby by the elbow and propelled him along the street. The man blinked, focused his gaze down his aquiline nose, and regarded the viscount in mild surprise. "Ashtead," he pronounced in delighted accents. "Was I expecting to see you?"

"Not in the least." Ashtead kept his friend moving. "How is your current play progressing?"

Jacoby beamed at him. "Very well, very well indeed. Only I cannot quite determine how to end the first act." He halted, that dreamy expression creeping once more into his eyes. "Tell me, do you think the colonel really ought to accuse Wallsingham of being a thief and a villain, or do you think it better to keep the audience in suspense?" He shook his head. "It has been troubling me for the last three days."

"As I have not the least notion what your current effort is about, I cannot judge," Ashtead assured him. "Have you been wandering about Brighton quoting your dialogue again?"

"Have I?" Jacoby blinked at him. "Upon my word, *do* I do that?"

Ashtead smiled, a feat of which he had not thought himself capable a bare quarter of an hour before. Jacoby, when between plays, was the best of good fellows, particular in all matters of dress and society, a bruising rider to hounds and a devil to go. But let the muse but come upon him, and only the efforts of whatever exasperated manservant he currently employed assured that he either ate or kept his appointments. From the looks of him, Ashtead was willing to wager that his latest valet had handed in his notice and not yet been replaced.

With an obvious effort, Jacoby pulled himself together. "Sorry, old fellow, you know how it is with me. I can usually remember, if I make the effort." His countenance, always remarkable more for its amiability than any perfection of feature, now glowed with goodwill. "But—did I know you were summering here?"

"I'm not." Yet the idea suddenly appealed to Ashtead. Guilt plagued him over driving Edwina from the only home she knew. Of course, no one could doubt Lady Xanthe's eminent respectability, or her complete capability of chaperoning the chit, yet he could not rid himself of the feeling he ought to remain for a little while. That Edwina didn't want him around, she had made abundantly clear. Yet he felt it to be a matter of pride that she should come to realize he was sincere in his disinterest in her.

The hesitation must have shown in his countenance, for Jacoby's grin widened. "Why not stay a week or so? Be glad of your company. There's a troubling bit in the first scene I'd be glad to have someone hear. I'm putting up at the Castle Inn, I think." He considered a moment, then nodded. "Yes, the Castle Inn. Be glad to accompany you back to inquire about a room."

Somehow, that decided it. The two strolled along the street together, and Ashtead's ill temper faded beneath the pressing discussion over a hero whose every action was wrathfully misinterpreted by his lady's father. In a surprisingly short time they entered the inn.

But there Ashtead met with a setback. The rooms, the clerk explained with obsequious dismay, had all been bespoken weeks before. There were, in fact, no accommodations to be found at all in Brighton, not there, not at the Old Ship, nor at any of the other smaller establishments to be found in the vicinity. And since he had sent a man around only that morning to enquire of the rental agents, he was forced to disclose that not a single lodging remained either.

"You can share mine," Jacoby suggested with that amiability that won him so many friends, despite his vagaries and tendency to quote his current work.

As fond of his friend as Ashtead was, he had his limits. He considered, and the obvious solution rushed to his mind. "I believe I have an aunt staying here. I'll let you know." He thanked the clerk, nodded an absent farewell to Jacoby, and exited the establishment.

His maternal aunt, Mrs. Hester Winslow, relict of a brusque but openhanded country squire, would not turn him away. For some reason he had never been able to fathom, she had always cherished a fondness for him, regarded him with a tolerant amusement even when the rest of the family threatened to wash their hands of him. He retraced his steps, looking forward to seeing his relative again.

She had taken the same house on the Marine Parade every summer for the last two dozen years or more. He'd visited her there upon several occasions, when his youthful indiscretions had made it advisable for him to seek a temporary refuge. He hadn't a doubt he'd find her there. And more amazingly, he hadn't a doubt she'd take him in once more. His rapid steps carried him past the door where Edwina and Lady Xanthe had taken up residence, past three more houses, then up the front steps of the familiar residence next in line. He knocked, a minute passed, then a footstep sounded in the tiled entry and the door opened.

The familiar, portly figure of Edgarth, the butler who had tended his maternal aunt for as long as Ashtead could remember, filled the frame. The man stared at him, blinked, and the polite expression faded to a reproving, but resigned, frown. "We were not expecting you, my lord."

"I didn't know I was coming. Is my aunt at home?"

"If you will come this way—" Edgarth began.

Ashtead waved him aside. "In the salon? Save your weary bones, I'll find her." He crossed the passage and opened the door to the bright, sunny room where his aunt loved to spend her mornings.

A woman of advancing middle age sat in a padded chair by the window, a book open in one hand, a lorgnette held in the other to enable her to read. Silver touched the brown curls that ran riot beneath a frivolous lace cap adorned with ribands and silk roses. Her comfortably plump figure was displayed to advantage in a green muslin morning gown in the high kick of fashion.

He swept off his low-crowned beaver and stepped forward, head lowered in the posture of a supplicant. In apologetic tones, he said, "The black sheep has come calling, Aunt Hester."

She looked up, and her eyes brightened. Casting the book aside, she started to her feet. Ashtead crossed the room in four steps, forestalling her, dropping a kiss on her curls. "Dearest boy!" She stood on tiptoe to kiss his cheek. "How good of you to call. Are you staying here?"

The last remnants of his morning's irritation didn't stand a chance. He grinned at her. "If you'll have me. The town is booked to the last room."

"And you never thought to make arrangements in time, I suppose." She sighed in an exaggerated manner. "If that isn't exactly like you."

"Most likely," said a dry, female voice from behind him, "he had no idea the lady he was currently pursuing would be coming here."

He spun about to see the tall, slender figure of his younger sister standing in the doorway, dressed in a simple morning gown of shell-pink muslin, which set off her glossy brown ringlets. "What the devil are you doing here, Lydia?" he demanded.

Laughter burst from her. "Odious creature, is that any

way to greet me? What has it been? A month, at the very least." She glided forward.

He shook his head as he went to her, taking her hand and kissing her cheek. "Two weeks ago, at the Somersbys' ball. Don't tell me you've forgotten? I even complimented your gown."

"Now, that's doing it too brown. I'd remember so rare an event."

"No, I recall it distinctly. I said something about your finally putting off your half-mourning, and you said how widowhood suited you exactly."

"Well, it does. But before you decide to inflict yourself on dearest Aunt Hester, be advised that your niece and nephew are staying in this house as well."

He did his best to look revolted, though in truth he had a fondness for little Anne, who had reached the distinguished age of three years. Gregory, Lord Harcourt, a mere infant at eighteen months, elicited less pleasure in him, though he felt certain he would like him well enough in another year's time.

"They will hardly bother you at all," Aunt Hester assured him. "She has brought their nurserymaid, of course, and their expeditions to the seaside leave them so exhausted they sleep most of the time they are in the house."

Lydia sank onto the sofa with practiced grace. "So what has brought you to Brighton? A female, of course. That goes without saying. Who is it this time?"

"Edwina," he said, and took a certain satisfaction in the puzzled look that crossed his sister's face.

"Edwina," she murmured, then her eyes widened. "Do you—no, you *cannot* mean *Cousin* Edwina. Do you?"

Ashtead inclined his head.

"But— Do you mean Great-Uncle Sylvester has actually let the poor girl out of the Castle?"

"She ran away." Best be honest about it at once, for he knew Lydia well enough to know his sister would ferret out the truth.

Lydia struggled for a moment to look properly shocked, then abandoned the attempt. "Well, it's dreadful, of course, but try as I might, I cannot blame her. But what has her presence in Brighton to do with you?"

He assumed an air of nonchalance he was far from feeling. "Oh, I'm the reason she ran away. It seems she took exception to her grandfather's plans to force us to wed."

"To—" Lydia blinked at him.

Aunt Hester laid her hand on his arm. Humor lit her warm gray eyes. "She ran away from you, and you, wicked one, immediately pursued her to her place of refuge? How shocking."

"Isn't it?" he agreed. "She's staying with her godmother, Lady Xanthe Simms. Are you acquainted with her?"

"Why, yes," said Aunt Hester, then a slight frown creased her brow. "Though I cannot at the moment remember when last I had the pleasure of seeing her. I shall pay her a morning visit, of course. Now," she added as the door opened and Edgarth entered bearing a tray of refreshments, "make yourself comfortable, and I will order a room prepared for you. Have you any idea how long you will honor us with your company?"

He grinned at the irony of her words. "None in the least. I knew I could count on you."

He stayed long enough to drink a glass of wine, then took his leave of them. He would have to return to the Old Ship, where he had stabled his curricle and pair. He would drive his portmanteau and valet to his aunt's home, then— His steps slowed. Just what would he do? Pass the time with his various acquaintances, he supposed. Listen to excerpts from Jacoby's play. Escort his sister and aunt to a round of parties. That would ensure his seeing Edwina as well.

And he wanted to see her. Or rather, he wanted her to see him. See him paying court to other ladies perhaps. Let her know he had no further interest in her in the least. And while he was at it, it wouldn't hurt him to keep an eye on the chit as well. She was, after all—at least in the eyes of the world—the heiress to the vast Shoreham fortune. In her innocence and inexperience, she might well fall prey to some damned fortune hunter. And if that occurred, he would hold himself very much to blame.

He had hoped to spend this first evening talking over old times with Sir William Jacoby with the aid of several bottles of some prime vintage of burgundy, but his sister soon put paid to this plan. She and Aunt Hester planned to attend a party at Lady Westhaven's, and as his loving aunt informed him, he could earn his keep by escorting them. Resigned to this fate, he dressed with his usual care, then descended the stairs to find his aunt already waiting in the salon.

He raised the quizzing glass that hung about his neck on a black silk riband and subjected her to a detailed scrutiny. She had arrayed herself in a gown of green silk, embellished with a single flounce, and a head of ostrich plumes and lace, all dyed to match. The Winslow emeralds glittered at her throat and ears. "Ravishing," he announced when his study had taken in the silk slippers that completed the outfit.

She examined her appearance in the mirror that hung

above the hearth. "Yes," she said after a considering moment. "I am quite pleased with it. And don't try to flummery me. I know perfectly well you have no interest in such fripperies. If I give you a detailed account of every item I am wearing, it will be nothing less than you deserve for your insincerity."

"You wrong me!" he protested, laughing.

"Indeed you do. It is well known he takes far too much interest in the ladies." Lydia swept into the room, a vision in pale yellow gauze trimmed with blond lace.

He raised his quizzing glass again, and nodded approval. "Your mourning didn't suit you nearly so well."

Her nose wrinkled in distaste. "It didn't suit me in the least. A year in black gloves for that—" She broke off. "Never mind. I am free of him, that is what matters." She cast a sideways glance at Ashtead as she drew on her gloves. "And I have a great desire to sing some soulful ballad this night."

Ashtead, who had reached for his aunt's shawl, which lay across a chair, froze. "Do you mean you're dragging me to some musical *soiree?*"

Lydia burst out laughing. "If you could but see your face, Ashtead. Yes, there is to be music, and I hope a very great deal of it. And you cannot tell me you will not enjoy it, for that I will never believe."

"Let us say I enjoy well-played music." He arranged Aunt Hester's shawl about her plump shoulders and offered her his arm. Would Edwina be there? he wondered. If so, it could well be her first party. He found himself looking forward to seeing her reactions.

They walked, as the Westhavens lived only three doors away. Lights filled the windows, but as yet no strains of music drifted through the air to challenge the soft roar of the ocean waves. He greeted his host and hostess, acknowledged with reserve the introduction to the daughter of the household, who eyed him with more speculation than he found comfortable, saw his aunt and sister into the company of their friends, and slipped away on his own to survey the assembled company.

On the far side of the room he noted two of his cronies, both vying for the favor of the dusky-haired Miss Fanny Marlowe, an heiress whose fortune far outweighed the plainness of her features. For a moment he toyed with the idea of cutting out his friends, for Miss Marlowe's taste ran to exalted titles, and she had made it clear that the heir to the Marquis of Shoreham would suit her and her considerable resources quite well. And her resources would suit him, he reflected with a sudden savage anger. Lord, had his great-uncle reduced him to the paltry ranks of the fortune hunters? Miss Marlowe might be grooming herself for a great position, but Ashtead could not like the ambitious gleam in her eye.

He turned away in time to see a regal matron of medium height enter the room. The next moment he recognized her as Lady Xanthe Simms. A tall, elegant young lady followed in her wake, her slender figure set off by a half robe of pale peach-colored gauze open over an underdress of ivory silk. She had swept her light brown hair into a knot on the top of her head, and her long curls fell in clusters past her shoulders. Lord, what a difference in the chit. This ravishing miss bore no resemblance whatsoever to the gawky female he had glimpsed through a drunken haze in her grandfather's chamber.

"What a clever imitation you are doing of a stuffed trout," Lydia's voice whispered in his ear. "Whomever are you gawking at?"

He cast her a fulminating glare. "I was merely startled

to see how considerable an alteration can be brought about by a touch of modishness. Do you not recognize our Cousin Edwina?"

Lydia blinked. "Edwina? Where?" Then, when Ashtead pointed her out; "No, you are bamming me! Was she not a drab little thing?"

Even as she spoke, Aunt Hester hurried toward the two new arrivals, hands extended. "Lady Xanthe! What a delight it is to see you again. It has been far too long."

An irrepressible dimple showed in Xanthe's cheek. "Far too long indeed," she declared. "But you must allow me to present my goddaughter."

Ashtead strolled over to join them. "You must remember my Cousin Edwina," he said to his aunt. He greeted Xanthe, then turned to observe Edwina gazing about the room, her gray eyes bright, her full lips slightly parted. "You must learn to cultivate an air of boredom, dear cousin," he said softly.

She eyed him with cool hostility. "Why should I? I have longed to go to parties, and I intend to enjoy every moment of it!"

"And so you should." Lydia held out both her hands. "Dearest Cousin Edwina, you will not remember me, but I have the misfortune to be Ashtead's sister."

Edwina's countenance brightened. "My Cousin Lydia! But I do not remember you being so beautiful."

Lydia laughed. "My dear, we shall be the greatest friends, I just know it, for you have never before been in society, and I am only just emerged from mourning. Oh, I cannot tell you how glad I am you escaped that wretched Castle. Ashtead has been telling me his part in this dreadful affair, and I was never more shocked. Men," she added, directing a withering look at her brother, "are such beasts!"

Ashtead frowned at his sister. "Rather an exaggeration, do you not think?"

"No! Only consider how you treated poor Edwina, both you and Great-Uncle Sylvester. And as for your behavior in general—!" She turned back to Edwina. "He has the most shocking reputation, you must know."

Edwina regarded him for a long moment. "Indeed."

A sudden, impish light glowed in Lydia's eyes. "You may not credit it, but he can charm a bird from the trees, if he puts his mind to it."

"You are quite right. I cannot credit it."

Ashtead fixed his sister with a quelling eye. "If you two ladies are quite through vilifying me?"

"We have barely begun," Lydia informed him, her tone teasing. "If he continues to pursue you," she added to Edwina, "just send him about his business. It might take a while, but he will eventually take the hint. And you will certainly not lack for suitors."

"Oh, no," Edwina said quickly. "I am not hanging out for a husband. I cannot think of a worse fate than to be forever under the domination of some man."

Lydia clasped her hands in delight. "Those are precisely my own sentiments! My dear, we shall deal famously together!" She tucked her arm through Edwina's and drew her off, their heads bending close together in a rush of confidence.

Ashtead watched their retreat, torn between exasperation at his sister's teasing and an unexpected irritation at being excluded.

Eddie strolled through the salon of the elegant town house on the Steyne, rented for the summer by Lord and Lady Trevelian. It still amazed her how many people welcomed her—and Lady Xanthe—into their homes, as if they had known Xanthe all their lives. The musical *soiree* at the Westhavens' two nights ago, then that elegant dinner party at the home of the Dowager Lady Forth, and tonight a card party.

A card party. A thrill of excitement raced up her spine. Tonight, she would begin the slow process of winning her independence. And she wouldn't let this sudden rush of nerves interfere.

She stopped to exchange greetings with Miss Fanny Marlowe, a plain-faced young lady with a drive within her that Eddie could feel as a tangible force. Miss Marlowe was likely to get what she wanted, though Eddie wondered just what that might be. She paused again by an elderly woman with a keen eye and hearty laugh. She didn't want to race to the gaming tables. She had to take this slowly if she wanted to come out of her adventure with her reputation in tact.

The ormolu clock on the mantel showed that a good half hour had passed since she'd arrived. Time, she decided, and braced her nerve.

Several gentlemen had just entered the card room. She would follow, watch the play for a few minutes, see if anyone to whom she had been introduced would ask her to join him in a hand. Only, she didn't want to win money from people she knew. An excess of scruples, she realized, might well prove her undoing.

Ten tables were crowded into the drawing room, three seating five or more, seven set for two. Those, she knew, would be devoted to piquet. And she wasn't the only lady to pursue this enjoyable pastime. Several already sat opposite gentlemen. She positioned herself near one of these and waited, regretting that propriety prevented her from approaching a potential partner.

She still waited some twenty minutes later, her spirits sinking lower and lower, when a hearty laugh drew her attention. A very large gentleman, garbed in an elegant coat accented with a truly remarkable brocade waistcoat, stood in the doorway. Graying hair, styled in the latest fashion, set off his great beak of a nose and jutting chin . . . Eddie's eyes widened. She wended her way through the tables, staring at the gentleman, not quite able to believe what she saw.

"Uncle Marmaduke?" she asked as she reached his side.

The man, who had been surveying the room through a quizzing glass, turned it on her. The next moment it dropped, bouncing gently against his wide chest. "No," he declared. "It cannot be possible. My only niece was a poor little dab of a chit. You, my child, are a great beauty. And the very image of your dear mamma, God rest her soul." He grasped her hands. "Has that old devil let you out of his Castle fortress at last? I'd despaired of ever laying eyes upon you again."

She returned the warm grip, and found her eyes misting with tears. "Uncle Marmaduke," she repeated. "It is so very good to see you."

He dropped a kiss on her forehead. "Here, this is no place to talk. Come with me." Still holding one of her hands, he led her from the room and across the hall to the front salon, where a number of people sat in small groups, conversing. He drew her down on a small sofa and settled at her side. "What's it been, nine years? Well, you've got a lot to tell me then. How have you gone on?"

She did tell him, stumbling over the early part of her story, over the time following the death of her parents. He listened in silence until she related her flight from the Castle; then a great guffaw of laughter escaped him. "Serves the old rascal right, after keeping you a virtual prisoner like that. So you reached your godmamma safely, I'm glad to see. And what will you do now?"

She glanced about to make sure no one overheard. "I intend to win sufficient funds to become independent."

He stared at her, his smile broadening into a wide grin. "My own dear niece." He chuckled. "Lord, that will have old Shoreham fuming."

Eddie hunched a shoulder. "I don't care."

"That's the spirit." He beamed at her, all approval. "Though it ain't easy to keep the dibs in tune, m'dear."

"No." She squeezed his hand. "Under the hatches?"

"Always, m'dear. Always." He grinned again, the expression oddly boyish on a face lined from so many late nights at the gaming tables. "What will you do if you lose?"

"I won't." She couldn't allow herself to consider that possibility. "In fact"—and she forced a smile—"I can teach you a few tricks. I haven't been idle these nine years past, you know. I've learned a thing or two."

"That's my girl." He reached up to ruffle her curls, then seemed to think better of it. "I shall look forward to seeing you in action."

"Which is where I might need your help. I don't know any gentlemen."

He surged to his feet. "Let us go and have a look at 'em."

They returned to the card room, where he raised his quizzing glass and allowed it to rest on first one gentleman, then another. "No," he muttered. "Lord, no, not that one." The glass moved on until suddenly Uncle Marmaduke allowed it to drop. "The very man," he announced softly. "Best test your abilities on someone who's capable, and who'll play for a pittance. Don't want to lose your entire stake if you find you're not up to snuff."

She most assuredly did not. Obediently, she followed her uncle across the room, standing slightly aside as he approached an elderly gentleman of military bearing.

"Colonel Chesterfield." Marmaduke Rutland gestured toward a table that for the moment stood empty. "Will you honor me with a hand?"

"What, currently flush?" demanded the colonel with jovial pleasure.

The two took their places. Eddie moved close, and was pleased, for her uncle's sake, to hear the meager stakes suggested by Chesterfield. The man showed a fine mastery of the game as well; he made his decisions quickly, played with care, and came out the winner.

"Would you care for your revenge?" inquired the colonel, and collected the cards to shuffle once more.

Uncle Marmaduke looked up at Eddie and winked. "Have you met my niece? No? Then allow me to present Lady Edwina Langston."

The colonel rose, but a slight frown creased his brow. "Langston," he murmured. "You'd be Shoreham's granddaughter?" Eddie acknowledged it, and the colonel nodded. "Delighted. Do you share your grandfather's passion for piquet?"

And there was her opening. Under her uncle's humorous eye, Eddie replaced him at the table.

This was only a trial, she reminded herself. She needed to know if she were really as good as she believed. If not—Well, Uncle Marmaduke was right. She had best find out playing for low stakes.

She was on edge, she realized, suffering a terrible attack of nerves. She hesitated, then mastered herself sufficiently to play with her normal concentration. Each card proved an agony, but as the play continued, she found more and more tricks going to her. She took the last, declared the score she had tracked carefully, and the colonel laughed.

"I make that—" He broke off, musing, then shook his head. "Eleven shillings." With a sigh, he heaved himself to his feet. "A delightful hand, my dear Lady Edwina. It has been a great pleasure to have made your acquaintance." He nodded to Marmaduke Rutland and made his way across the room.

Eddie looked up at her uncle. "I won."

His smile spread from ear to ear. "Capital, m'dear. You do me credit, you do. Learned your lessons well."

She managed a shaky smile. "I have never been so frightened!"

Marmaduke shook his head. "Didn't show it in the least. And don't you let your fears hold sway over you, or you'll succumb to foolish mistakes. Always keep a cool head."

She nodded. "With whom should I play next?"

Marmaduke scanned the room and frowned. "There's—" He broke off. "No, never do for you to play with him. Nor him," he added musingly as his gaze continued to rove. "Certainly not Kennilworth. They say he never loses. Dash it," he added after a moment, "can't see anyone I'd recommend."

"Oh." She felt deflated. After bracing her courage sufficiently to launch her new career, it proved a sore blow to have it end so abruptly for the night.

Accepting the inevitability of it, she drew Miss Fanny Marlowe into a hand. They played for penny points, and after a game of six hands, Eddie found herself ahead by only a little over a pound. The case proved the same with the next three ladies whom she drew into games. When she at last took her leave of the party with Lady Xanthe, her depression far outweighed her elation. ability to herself; she had indeed won. a scant five pounds. That, she decided her not only a card sharp, but a pretty at that. She had proved her But she had gained in disgust, made. unsuccessful one at that.

Four

Eddie sat on a wooden bench and gazed across the sand to the waves that lapped the shore. Beyond, no bigger than tiny specks, bobbed the fishing dories that had set forth before dawn. Overhead the gulls cried, the breeze blew crisp and cool with salt tang, and the sun warmed her back. Eddie was utterly miserable.

The slightest change stirred in the air. The scent of violets wafted toward her on the wings of innumerable butterflies that suddenly surrounded her. Daffodils sprang from the sand, bobbing their yellow heads in time to the melody of a flute.

"Lovely," she said perfunctorily.

The colorful wings fluttered as the butterflies formed the outline of a figure. They grew, expanded, then exploded in a shower of sparkles to reveal Xanthe, dressed in a pale blue morning gown, standing at their center. "Why should you be depressed?" the fairy godmother demanded. "Last night was only your first attempt."

A shaky sigh escaped Eddie. "I could only play with ladies. It's true, of course, there are ladies who will play for high stakes, but my uncle has assured me I may not game with them for fear of being labeled fast. He seemed quite certain that would be a terrible fate."

"It would," agreed Xanthe, an amused smile playing

about her lips. A rounded feather drifted in lazy swirls to the sand.

"And if I confine myself to only the most respectable females, I cannot hope to win as much as one hundred pounds, when I need ten thousand."

Xanthe seated herself on the bench. "Then it is clear you must play with gentlemen."

Eddie shook her head. "I don't know any. And because of my age, the very few I shall meet will undoubtedly humor me, as did Colonel Chesterfield, and insist upon playing for penny points."

"No," agreed Xanthe, "that would never do."

Eddie glared at her. "Have you no suggestions? I will not return to the Castle in defeat!"

"Of course you shall not. You must merely meet the right gentlemen."

"But how am I to do that?" she demanded. "One can hardly consider Uncle Marmaduke's acquaintances to be suitable—or flush enough in the pocket, for that matter."

Xanthe gazed out over the ocean, where the dories drew closer. After a moment, she said, "He is not the only gentleman of your acquaintance currently in Brighton."

"No!" The word exploded from Eddie. "I will not—I *cannot* ask Ashtead for aid."

"It would not be for aid exactly." Xanthe continued to gaze toward the sea. "He need know nothing about your purpose."

"No!" Eddie repeated.

A sigh escaped Xanthe. "My love, only consider—"

"No." Eddie rose. "I will have nothing to do with Ashtead!"

"Even if you could contrive to win a portion of your independence from him and his friends?"

Eddie shook her head. "I will have nothing to do with him. And if my running away has indeed cost him my grandfather's fortune, he has not a penny to spare on gaming."

"But he has friends."

Eddie's gaze narrowed on her fairy godmother. "You wish me to spend time with him!" she accused.

The fairy brushed an invisible speck of dust from her gown. "Nonsense, my love."

"But you do!" Eddie's hands clenched into fists. "How could you? Or have you tricked me, and been in league with my grandfather all along? Has this been an elaborate ruse to make me believe I have no other option than to marry Ashtead? Well, it will not work! I will not marry him, I will not ask his help, I will not even speak with him!" She turned on her heel, which proved no easy task on the soft sand, and marched back toward the house.

An empty, disoriented sensation assailed her, as if she had just fallen a great distance and her stomach had yet to catch up to her. If she could not trust Xanthe, what would become of her? Where could she go?

She had taken no more than a dozen steps before the incredible bulk of Titus shimmered down the stairs of their house. He stalked majestically across the street and stopped in front of her, gazing up at her with his immense blue eyes.

"Are you in on this too?" Eddie demanded. A heaviness filled her chest and throat, her eyes stung, and only with an effort did she keep her chin from trembling.

Titus opened his mouth in a silent, but definitely reproving, meow. After a moment's gazing at her, he rubbed against her leg, then wrapped himself around first one of her ankles, then the other.

Eddie stooped, picked up his hefty bulk, and stroked the long white fur. "No, you wouldn't have anything to do with this, would you?"

Titus fixed her with a penetrating stare.

"She wouldn't either?" Eddie regarded the cat, frowning. Had she overreacted? She had to admit that where Ashtead was concerned, she was not wholly reasonable at the moment. Perhaps she should make use of him. After all, this was, in a sense, his fault. He might as well help her to her independence. As Xanthe had said, he didn't have to know what she was about.

Tonight, she reflected, there would be an informal party, and Xanthe had implied that cards would be the primary entertainment. Perhaps—

She dressed with care in an elegantly simple gown of jonquil muslin trimmed with ivory lace. She could grow accustomed to wearing beautiful gowns, attending amusing parties, living this life of luxury. But she could not allow herself to. That would mean marrying Ashtead— though she suspected her grandfather must be angry enough with her by now that even this ultimate show of submission would not reinstate her. No, she had made the best possible decision for her future, and tonight she would take positive steps toward achieving it.

When she descended the stairs, she found Xanthe ahead of her, dressed in her favorite blue with a cap of lace and riband roses perched amid her plaited hair. "Lovely, my dear." Xanthe beamed at her. "Except—"

The fairy hummed a soft bar of music, and four roses, two of yellow and two of white, appeared before her. Tiny white blossoms peeked from the lace that held this confection together. She waved her hand, and Eddie felt it settle among her curls.

Xanthe walked around her, observing the result, and nodded in satisfaction. "Now we are ready. Have you made your plans for tonight?"

Eddie nodded. "Ashtead it will have to be, I fear."

Xanthe patted her hand. "It will do very well, my love. He knows everyone, and he will only introduce you to those who will neither cheat nor bandy your name about in clubs."

Eddie made no reply. She knew dangers lurked along this path she had chosen; she only hoped she could escape more or less unscathed—and with the competence she needed.

She spotted Ashtead almost as soon as they arrived. In his black coat of exquisite cut, set off by his broad shoulders, he looked every inch the Corinthian. Well, she knew him for a rake. It would be an odd thing indeed if he did not cultivate an appearance that sent feminine pulses pounding and induced sighs of longing. She only wished the arrogant beast did not affect her in that manner.

It wasn't as if he worked his wiles on her. At the moment, in fact, he had not the least notion she had arrived. He stood at the opposite side of the salon, deep in conversation with a rather odd but amiable-looking gentleman. His companion's unkempt appearance made him stand out dreadfully amidst society's elegant elite, yet she did not dismiss him out of hand. He stood barely above medium height, his features pleasant if his expression somewhat distracted, and his coat was of exquisite cut, even if worn with an air of nonchalance.

"Do you think he might do?" Xanthe murmured in her ear.

Eddie shook her head. "He seems an unusual companion for anyone as fastidious as Ashtead. And even if he should prove to be as rich as Croesus, and addicted to piquet, I can hardly stroll over and request an introduction. Ashtead and I are not precisely upon the best of terms."

From the opposite side of the room, Lydia waved to her. An elderly woman sat at her side, talking without cease. Lydia broke across her flowing words with an apology, sprang to her feet, and hurried over. "I am so glad you have come," she exclaimed. "Lady Melbourne was my husband's godmamma, you must know, and the dearest creature, but she will talk so! I feared I should never escape."

"You must cultivate the art of the tactful retreat," came Ashtead's voice from behind Eddie.

He had a pleasant voice, Eddie noted, deep, with an undercurrent of amusement. It seemed shockingly out of character. She turned as he greeted Xanthe, and found he was not alone. Beside him stood the peculiar gentleman she had noticed with him before.

"And what of you, Cousin Edwina?" Ashtead's coolly polite smile came to rest on her. "Are you finding Brighton to your liking?"

If he intended to be civil, so much the better. She tried a friendly smile. "I only regret I know so few people."

"Then permit me to help remedy that. May I present to you Sir William Jacoby?"

"What?" His companion started out of the reverie into which he had fallen. "Pleasure, of course." He nodded to each of them, but his gaze settled on Lydia. "Interesting face," he pronounced after a moment. "You don't read poetry, do you?"

Lydia stiffened. "I beg your pardon?"

"Poetry," Jacoby repeated. "Just that you put me in mind of my heroine, and she's forever quoting *Marmion.*"

"Your—" Lydia cast a helpless glance at her brother.

"Jacoby is a playwright," he explained. "And deep in the throes of creation at the moment. I dragged him physically from his room tonight, but I fear I forgot to bring his mind as well."

Jacoby grinned, his dreamy eyes showing a flash of shrewd intelligence. "Beg your pardon. I'm quite presentable ordinarily, but as Ashtead says, when I'm writing, I can't seem to keep a grasp on the real world."

Lydia regarded him in fascination. "Can you not leave such trumpery matters to your valet or some other servant?"

"There's the rub." He looked sheepish. "The last fellow couldn't put up with me any longer. It's been about three weeks now, and I can't seem to keep anything in order."

"Good heavens." Lydia looked to her brother. "Can you not send Ottley around to him? Or perhaps have him engage a new valet for the poor man?"

"Ottley." Jacoby nodded. "Lord, yes. Why didn't I think of the man? He's just the sort of character I need in the last act." And with that, he dragged a small notebook from an inner pocket of his coat, muttered something about being in need of a pen, and wandered off.

Lydia stared after him, bemused. "How did you ever contrive to bring him to a card party?"

"Oh, he's a great one for piquet," Ashtead said. "He thought a night out might clear the clutter of his thoughts."

"I can't say it appears to have done him any good,

so far. But Ashtead, only look at his coat! And as for his neckcloth—!" Lydia shook her head. "The poor man needs someone to look after him. There, he's just standing in the center of the room as if he's forgotten what he set out to do. Really, Ashtead." With a shake of her head, she set forth after Jacoby and took his arm, guiding him toward a doorway.

"The maternal instinct." Ashtead turned his rueful gaze to Eddie. "You might not believe it at the moment, but Jacoby is quite good company."

"You said he enjoys piquet?" She dared not look at Ashtead, lest he detect how much this topic meant to her. "I should dearly love a game myself." There, she'd gotten it out; now to see if he would rise to her fly.

Ashtead looked revolted. "I should have thought you tired of that pastime. You cannot tell me you have not played it every evening for as long as you can remember."

"It only grows boring when one plays against the same opponent night after night. I know every one of Grandfather's tricks, as he knows mine." She risked a glance at him. "You can have no idea how I have longed to test my skill against other people."

A genuine smile tugged at his mouth, and the charm of so simple an expression left her confused. What business had he to disarm her so utterly, and with so little effort? It was absurd, and so was she. Of course he was charming. If he weren't, he could never have developed such a reputation as a rake.

His disconcerting smile remained. "Will you honor me with a game?"

She hesitated, reluctant to spend time in his company. Yet try as she might, she could think of no graceful way to avoid the invitation. And she did not want to offend him—at the moment, at least. He might prove useful to her. With what show of grace she could muster, she accepted his proffered arm and accompanied him to the drawing room, where tables had been arranged.

Several people stood around one of these, where two gentlemen played piquet, their expressions intent. One, in his early thirties and bearing the stamp of a military man, seemed vaguely familiar. It was on the tip of her tongue to ask Ashtead the man's identity, when his opponent supplied it.

"You win again, Kennilworth," the man declared as he threw down his last card. "Damme, but you've the devil's own luck."

Kennilworth. Uncle Marmaduke had pointed him out, saying he never lost. And from the amount of money that now exchanged hands, he played for high stakes. Somehow, she must contrive an introduction to him. Her speculative gaze moved to Ashtead. She would have to move slowly, not raise his suspicions, but with or without his help, she would meet Kennilworth.

Ashtead, ignorant of her intentions, drew out a chair for her, then took the seat opposite. A new deck rested on the cloth, and he broke it open and sorted out the lower pips. "For what stakes would you care to play?"

"Whatever you wish." She accompanied the response with a beguiling smile.

His hands slowed, then continued their shuffling. "My great-uncle, as I remember, is a master of the game."

Eddie inclined her head. "He has some skill."

"You would say you have more?"

"I would never boast."

His eyes gleamed. "Far better to prove yourself, is it not?" He dealt the first of the cards. "As I believe both our pockets are wholly to let, shall we play for penny points?"

With this she agreed, for she could do nothing else, but she had the satisfaction of seeing his eyebrows rise as she took trick after trick.

"You've learned to play a tolerably fair game," he said.

"Fair?" She bristled. "I defeated you quite soundly!"

He regarded her with exaggerated disapproval. "You must learn not to crow over victories, for you never know of what feats your opponent might truly be capable."

"Are you trying to imply that you let me win?"

He smiled. "Oh, no. The luck was definitely with you."

"You mean the skill," she shot back. "I shall be only too happy to demonstrate it again, with another hand."

"Or I might permit you to pit your skill against Jacoby."

Eddie looked up to see Sir William standing near, watching their table. She studied him a moment, noting his alert expression, the intelligence that shone in his brown eyes. He did not seem in the least bemused or driven by the shades of his imagination now; he ought to be able to hold his own in a game. Nor, she decided, would a small loss at cards cause him the least concern or difficulty.

"I should be delighted." Sir William took Ashtead's place as the viscount rose.

To her relief, Ashtead answered a hail from some acquaintance and strolled across the room to join another game. Eddie turned back to her new opponent, to find him regarding her with a slight frown.

"You prefer to play for penny points?" he inquired, his tone polite but not enthusiastic.

"Only within the family. I imagine you would find it quite dull."

"Not if you should wish it," he said with real nobility if little truth.

"Then name whatever stakes you choose," she suggested.

They settled on shilling points, Eddie reflecting that if she lost, Xanthe would see to it that her purse contained sufficient funds to cover the sum. Only, she would have to pay her fairy godmother back, for the money at stake was hers, and hers alone. Well, she would just have to win.

She did, and found Sir William to be as charming a loser as he was avid a player. He promptly demanded first one rematch, and then another, and not once did he retreat into the world of his literary creations. When he rose from the table at last, it was with expressions of admiration for her abilities. In fact, the only flaw she could find in him was the he did not introduce her to any other gentlemen with whom she might continue her winning streak.

But she had won. And tomorrow night she would attend the public ball at the Castle Inn, and there would be a card room, and she would win again. She had made a start.

Her excitement over her accomplishment paled slightly in comparison to the thrill of her first ball. From the moment they entered the spacious chamber the next evening, Eddie's sight filled with the resplendent silks, laces, velvets, and jewels of the other attendees. And this, she reflected in a daze, was not even London, not the height of the Season. Only a public ball in the summer, in Brighton.

But she had the satisfaction of knowing herself as beautifully gowned as anyone present. Xanthe had spent considerable effort over her creation, selecting at last a half-robe of rose silk opened to reveal an under dress of white gauze trimmed with lace. Tiny roses decorated both the gown and Eddie's hair, and if she hadn't been certain the bees that buzzed about them were of Xanthe's providing, she would have rid herself of the flowers at once.

She wandered about the room, enjoying just being present, admiring the ladies' gowns, comparing the gentlemen to— The realization that she measured their appearance and demeanor against Ashtead came as a severe shock to her. The viscount might possess the more elegant figure, but almost any of these gentlemen must surpass him in amiability.

For that matter, she had not yet seen him this evening. Did he shun a public ball as beneath his notice? Yet surely his sister and aunt would demand his escort. She continued her progress about the room, now searching for a particular face, a particular pair of broad shoulders. Not that she really wanted to see him, of course, but she needed him to introduce her to potential card partners. Her disappointment at his absence only meant she might well waste one of her few precious chances to win her independence—from him.

Xanthe strolled at her side, all in soft blue silk with white lace and a fan of matching feathers. The sapphires clasped about her neck would have cost her a fortune, had she obtained them by conventional means. But there was little of the conventional about Xanthe. The fairy no longer walked, Eddie realized. She floated along, drawn by a team of miniature horses, their dainty hooves prancing a good two feet above the floor, their harness and plumes matching her own finery. Silk ribands served as their reins, and they left a trail of iridescent shod prints in the air that shimmered before evaporating. Eddie caught her lower lip between her teeth to keep herself from laughing as the tiny steeds cavorted amidst the crowd.

"Where do I begin?" she asked in a soft voice.

Xanthe hummed a quick bar, and a small card tied with a riband fluttered into Eddie's hand. "Why not with your first partner?"

Eddie looked around, and to her relief saw Sir William Jacoby making his way toward them. Perhaps Ashtead had sent his valet to him for the occasion, for Jacoby appeared quite elegant. Only the distracted expression in his eyes warned her his thoughts might not be altogether on his surroundings.

He bowed to Xanthe, then turned his rueful gaze on Eddie. "May I have the pleasure of this dance? I shall try very hard not to tread upon your feet." He offered her his arm. "Your cousins are not here this night?"

The question sounded a little too casual to her ears. She cast him a speculative glance, and saw that his gaze continually darted toward the door. She doubted it was Ashtead he wished to see. *No one* could be that desirous of seeing Ashtead. "I believe they plan to attend," she said, and to her fascination she saw a flicker of something that might have been either pleasure or relief in his eyes. Apparently, he had found Lydia's ministrations soothing.

They took their places in the line that formed, and she had no further time to contemplate Sir William's vagaries. She had to concentrate on the dance, for lack of opportunities to attend balls had caused the few steps she had learned from her last governess to fade from her memory. Luckily, Xanthe seemed to include dancing among the spells with which she blessed her godchildren, and Eddie acquitted herself quite creditably.

Not that Jacoby noticed. He suffered from severe distraction, twice coming to a halt, the gaze of his dreaming eyes unfocused. Eddie guided him through the movements, saw him safely to a corner where he could contemplate a possible ball scene for his play, then with relief turned to the young lieutenant Xanthe presented to her as a partner for the round dance that formed.

He pronounced himself more than willing to indulge her in a hand or two of piquet when the music ended, but he proved an indifferent player, preferring low stakes. "Not at all like casting the ivories," he informed her, and went on to regale her with tales of nights spent "rattling the bone box" for wagers that would have made Eddie's fortune in one evening.

She rose at last, anxious to make her escape, and found herself facing a young gentleman with a flamboyant waistcoat and intricately tied cravat. Whether it was his familiar manner or the knowing look in her eye, she could not be certain. She only knew she disliked him on sight.

"A lovely lady," he pronounced. "Introduce me," he commanded of her former partner.

Before Eddie could protest that she had no desire for this particular acquaintance, the officer presented Mr. Beverley Carradine to her. Much to her indignation, the officer then departed, leaving her facing the man. Without so much as asking her permission, Mr. Carradine took his vacated seat.

Eddie rose. "You—" she began, then broke off. Before her sat not the rakish young gentleman, but the knave of diamonds, exactly as he appeared on a deck of cards, complete with a thin line of reddish blond mustache. She blinked, but the illusion remained. From his sleeve fluttered an elaborately drawn queen of clubs, which swirled in ever larger circles as it neared the floor.

She sat down abruptly. "For what stakes do you play?" she inquired. The satisfaction on his face made her fingers itch to box his ears. With him, she need know no scruples about winning. How delightful of Xanthe to provide her with such an opponent.

Mr. Carradine reached across to capture her hand, his smile a trifle too knowing. A narrow hedge of thorns sprang up on the center of the cloth, its shoots spreading rapidly to create an impenetrable barrier. Carradine hesitated, a puzzled frown forming in his brow as if he had forgotten what he had intended to do; then he reached for the deck of cards.

"Are you feeling lucky this night?" he inquired, his confidence returning.

"Very," came her prompt response.

"Then let us play for stakes that will lend a little spice to the game."

Eddie agreed to his suggested sum, accepted the cards, made her discard, then watched him covertly. He displayed no hesitation, tossing cards onto the table with apparent unconcern, all the while keeping up a flirtatious chatter that struck Eddie as being too warm by half. By midway through the second hand she knew him for a trifling player, all dash and intimidation. His purpose seemed to center on captivating her rather than relieving her of what few funds she might possess.

As they finished their fourth hand, his sly jokes and

innuendos brought a flush to her cheeks, but his inept handling of the cards brought her score higher and higher. At the end of the game he compared their points, his expression one of utter disbelief. Numbly, he counted out the flimsies, which she stuffed into her reticule. The weight of almost three hundred pounds felt wonderful as it dangled from her wrist.

Mr. Carradine leaned forward, his nose brushing the thorns he could not see, but which effectively kept him from touching Eddie. "Would you care for some refreshment, my dear? Some champagne perhaps? We must toast this night, for it has brought us together."

"But not for long," came the cheerful but determined voice of Ashtead. "Cousin Edwina, your godmother has sent me in search of you."

She looked up, surprised to see him but grateful to be able to escape from Carradine's company. Still, it annoyed her that it was Ashtead who served as her excuse. She accepted the arm he offered.

His affability fell away as soon as they had moved from the table. "What the devil do you mean by playing with Carradine?" he demanded in a low tone.

Her eyebrows rose, and she turned to him with an expression of astonishment on her countenance. "I had no idea it was any concern of yours."

His teeth clenched. "Can you wonder I should be concerned? Since no one else has seen fit to warn you, pray allow me to say that Carradine is no fit companion for a green girl."

"It is quite unnecessary," she informed him loftily. "I had realized that within moments of laying eyes on him."

He halted. "Then what the deuce were you doing playing cards with him?"

"Winning." She shouldn't have said that, of course, but her pride and delight in her accomplishment bubbled within her, demanding an outlet.

"Winning," he repeated, his voice flat. "Not to mention damaging your reputation. Whatever possessed you?"

Her cheeks warmed. "It is hardly as bad as that," she responded, but could not keep a testy, defiant note from her voice.

"Could you not find a more suitable partner?"

"No!" she flared back. "I know very few people."

"You certainly came to know him."

"My last partner introduced him to me."

"He should have known better."

Eddie glared at him. "It is none of your concern."

"I beg to differ. You would not be here in Brighton if it were not for me—"

"That is certainly true' "

"—so I feel a certain responsibility for you," he continued without acknowledging her interruption.

"There is not the least need. I am under the protection of my fai—of my godmother, and need no one else to look after me. And I cannot believe she sent you after me!"

His lips twitched. "She did not. But it seemed the best thing to say at the moment."

She straightened to her full height and glared at him. "I do not require your interference."

"On the contrary, you seemed on the verge of going in search of champagne with that loose screw."

"I was going to do no such thing! I found his company repellent."

"Then why did you play cards with him?" he demanded.

She hesitated a fraction too long before she said, "He needed the set down of losing."

Ashtead's eyes narrowed. "That's not the only reason, is it? What are you about, my girl?"

"I am not your girl, and I am not about anything that need concern you."

"Ah." He drew the syllable out, his gaze resting on her face. "So you are doing something. Out with it, dear cousin."

She could feel her color heightening. "I am not your dear cousin either."

He waved aside her objection. "You cannot deny the cousin, though."

"Much as I should like to," she shot back.

The determined gleam remained in his eyes, but a muscle tugged at the corner of his mouth. "You will not succeed in distracting me, Cousin Edwina. What are you about?"

"What I choose to do is no concern of yours."

He turned to face her fully, and his hands gripped her shoulders. His grim expression caused her to try to draw back, but he did not release her.

"You are away from your home because of my da— wretched temper. And that, no matter how you try to deny it, makes me responsible. I will not allow you to come to any harm. Is that understood?"

She found it oddly difficult to breathe. "As I have no intention of coming to any harm," she managed, "the matter need not worry you."

"But it does." He released her. "Understand me, Edwina. If you do not tell me the truth of what you are about, I shall return you to your grandfather's house upon the instant. Is that clear?"

"I will not go with you!"

"You will not be able to prevent it," came his response, as simple as it was obviously true.

She must have looked mutinous, for he folded his arms and fixed her with a commanding glare. "Very well then. I will return you to your godmother's house right now, where you will pack your things. I will take you home immediately after breakfast in the morning. And do not think you can slip away and hide yourself, for you will not be able to. Whatever madness you are about is at an end."

Five

Ashtead watched the fury flash in Edwina's eyes, the tensing of her jaw as she bit back undoubtedly choice words. He felt a bit of a cad, but he was not about to let her see that. His fear that in her innocence—and rebellion—she might do herself serious harm haunted him.

She drew a deep breath. "If I do tell you, will that be the end of it? Will you promise me—*promise me*—not to take me back?"

He studied her, noting defiance, chagrin, frustration, and honest, desperate concern. It mattered to her. Whatever she was about was no lark but something of importance. He didn't want to betray her—in fact, he found himself in sympathy with her. After a long moment, he said, "On one condition. That if I cannot like what you are doing, you will permit me to afford you such protection as I can."

She regarded him, her expression dubious, obviously not trusting this response.

He burst out laughing. "My dear girl— No, I'm sorry, you do not like it when I call you that. But really, do you think me some sort of a monster?"

"Yes." The note of resentment sounded in her voice.

"Well, I am not. It's just that I'll not have you come

to any harm. But if that can be achieved without forcing you back to the Castle, then I'll be satisfied."

She studied his face, as if seeking confirmation of his words in his expression. At last she nodded. "I intend to become independent."

He frowned. "In what way?"

"In *every* way!" she exclaimed. "You are a man. You can have no idea what it is like to be wholly dependent for *everything* on a father, or grandfather, or brother, or husband." She said the last word with loathing. "I won't be forced to go somewhere, or to do something, or to marry simply because it pleases someone else that I should. I want to be able to say no if I wish to."

A muscle tugged at the corner of his mouth. "You said no to me."

"Yes, and only see the trouble it has caused. I have had to flee my home, for you may be certain Grandfather would force me to accept you."

"We all of us must do things from time to time that we would rather not," he pointed out.

She fixed him with a reproving stare. "If my grandfather were to cast you off right now, where would you sleep this night? From where would you get your next meal? You have your own properties," she went on before he could speak. "You are not wholly dependent upon the whims of another."

"No." He could think of any number of factors that bound him, but not at so basic a level. If he were indeed forced to look to his great-uncle—or anyone else, for that matter—for his every penny, he would find it unbearable. "But what," he said slowly, bringing the conversation back to his original purpose, "has that to say to your playing piquet with that profligate?"

"Everything." She looked up at him from beneath partially lowered lashes. "Can you not see? I *will* be independent. The only way to achieve that is by securing a competence."

He stared at her for a long moment while the significance of her words sank home. "Good God," he said, struggling between outrage and amusement. "Do you mean to say you hope to *win* this independence of yours?"

"But not as a common gamester," she hurried to assure him.

"No. I should think not," he declared with considerable feeling. "There is nothing *common* about you. But what if you lose?"

"You have played against me. Remember, it is all I have done, every evening, for as long as I can remember. Few gentlemen can claim the same."

It was true. She possessed a skill that could put hardened gamesters to shame. "But you cannot play against men such as that," he declared, voicing the thought aloud as it came to him.

"In truth," she said, with a sudden rush of candor, "I would rather not, for I could not like the tone of his conversation. But I know so very few gentlemen, and those I do know have no fortune they could stand to lose."

"A difficult situation, all in all," he agreed, his mind racing. "Have you confided your intentions to Mr. Rutland?"

A sudden, soft smile transformed the defiance in her features. "Dear Uncle Marmaduke. He is quite in sympathy with me, but not for all the goodwill in the world can he help me. He claims his acquaintances to be quite delightful, but not at all the sort to whom he can introduce me. And I very much fear he is right." Gamesters to a man, Ashtead would wager. It only amazed him that Rutland possessed so much discretion when it came to his niece. And that Edwina seemed willing to be guided by her disreputable uncle's judgment. But whether that showed innate good sense, or a susceptibility to rely too much on the opinions of others, he could not be certain.

If she insisted upon gaming, he would do best to take her in hand himself. It was a pity, of course, he did not possess sufficient fortune to hand over her longed-for competence; after all, it was he, his failure to refuse to offer for her in the first place, that had thrust her into her penniless predicament. Therefore, it was up to him to help her out of it before she fell into some serious scrape.

He cleared his throat. "I am acquainted with any number of gentlemen of respectable reputation who would not be the least the worse for losing a few hundreds to you. Some of them," he added with sudden feeling, "would be the better for the experience of losing to a female."

A light flickered in her eyes. "You mean you will help me? I thought—" She broke off.

He eyed her with misgivings. "What did you think?"

"Well, that when I had told you my plans, you would insist upon my returning to my grandfather upon the instant."

"But I gave you my word I would not."

"Yes, well—"

His brow lowered. "Do you really think so little of me that you believe I would go back on my given word?"

"I hardly know you," she pointed out. "And gentlemen seem to have such odd notions of honor."

Amusement stirred in him, and a deep chuckle broke

from his throat. "Brat," he said. "You're going to cause me a great deal of trouble and worry over the next few weeks, aren't you?"

He still considered her outlandish intentions the following morning as he stood on the shore. Behind him, he could hear his sister Lydia admonishing his niece not to throw sand at her little brother. He looked over his shoulder to where Lydia sat on a blanket, holding the stout infant Lord Harcourt in her arms. The children's nursemaid searched through her basket and brought out scoops and cups for little Anne to play with. The child at once started to pour measured spoonfuls of sand into the smallest cup. That should keep her happy for a while.

There were a number of other family groups enjoying the morning air, all with children of various ages. Already, Anne cast speculative glances at another little girl of about her own age, who cast shy glances back. It wouldn't be long before a friendship started. And speaking of friends, he saw Sir William Jacoby wandering aimlessly across the sand, gazing into space with that distracted expression that usually indicated he was hard at work on his current play. His appearance made it abundantly clear that the valet, secured for him only the previous day by Ottley, had already abandoned his post.

Lydia called to Jacoby; the man slowed, looked about, and seemed to become aware of his surroundings. After a moment, he wended his way across to her and bowed. "Lady Harcourt," he pronounced, as if dredging her name up from the depths of his mind.

"How goes your play?" she inquired, bestowing her benevolent smile on him. "Or did I do wrong in disturbing you?"

"Wrong? No, how could you? I am honored," he said, showing that his manners outweighed his honesty. He looked at the two children, both of whom regarded him with curiosity.

Ashtead strolled over to join them. "You have not met her brood, have you?" And he performed the introductions. Anne stood and made a clumsy curtsy in acknowledgment, and Sir William bowed once more. Then the girl bounded off toward the water with her nurse in pursuit.

"A delightful child." Sir William's gaze followed her. "Ashtead, why have I not written one into my play? Seeing Lady Harcourt with her children makes me feel certain my heroine ought to have a little girl."

"Would that not cause problems on stage?" Ashtead asked, watching his friend with amusement.

Jacoby shook his head. "I cannot see how I ever conceived of my Sophia without a child in her arms. My dear Lady Harcourt, I am much indebted to you." He held out his hand, and when Lydia tentatively took it, he carried her fingers to his lips, kissed them, then wandered off, murmuring, "Mary? Elizabeth? Katherine?" in an apparent attempt to hit upon the perfect name for the newest member of his cast.

"He does not mean to be rude," Ashtead informed his sister.

Lydia shook her head. "He is so very like a child himself, you know. All his attention on just one thing. Did he not like the valet Ottley found for him? He does so desperately need someone to watch over him."

"I fear Ottley might have had the wrong sort of servant in mind. It would take a rather special valet to deal with Jacoby."

Lydia considered. "Perhaps I should help. Do you think he would mind?"

"I doubt he would be aware of your assistance," came Ashtead's honest answer.

Lydia looked up the beach, where Jacoby's figure faded in the distance. "The poor, dear man. I shall set about it at once."

Ashtead averted his face so his sister should not see his amazement. He might have expected her to refer to Jacoby as an odd creature, or even feather-headed or cork-brained, but never as a poor, dear man. Jacoby stood in grave danger of being taken under Lydia's maternal wing.

The following night, when they attended the Audleys' *soiree,* the suspicion dawned on him that Jacoby had not the least objection to Lydia's solicitude. He arrived in his usual disorder, but the fact remained that he had indeed arrived. Ashtead had taken no steps to remind him of this invitation, as his friend had expressed the harassed desire to be permitted to spend an evening or two in solitude, at work on the current scene that plagued him. Yet here he was, at a respectably early hour, approaching them with eager steps.

Jacoby greeted them all, but retained his clasp on Lydia's hand. "I have given my Sophia a daughter, Lady Harcourt," he announced. "Would you do me the infinite kindness of telling me if my Arabella behaves in the manner of a real child?" He drew Lydia apart, already launching into his recital.

Lydia cast an uncertain glance over her shoulder at Ashtead and Aunt Hester, then looked back to Jacoby, her expression one of surprise. "Why, yes, that is exactly what she says!" she declared. Then; "No, never that." They settled on a small sofa, already deep in discussion.

Not far from them, Ashtead spotted Edwina standing beside the large, deceptively distinguished figure of her Uncle Marmaduke Rutland. She laughed at something the old gentleman said, and looked up at him with an expression of amused affection. A stab of annoyance shot through Ashtead. Why did she feel such loyalty for the old reprobate? His company did her no good. Of course, it did her little if any harm, a voice whispered in his mind. So why did Ashtead object?

"Because I don't want her associated with common gamesters," he muttered under his breath as he set off to detach her from that undesirable companionship.

As he neared, Rutland looked up, and he beamed at Ashtead. "Dear boy!" He stepped forward with both hands extended.

Ashtead found his grasped in a strong, enthusiastic grip. He returned the greeting, then looked beyond Rutland to see Edwina watching with an expression of hope mingled with uncertainty.

Rutland chuckled. "She's been waiting for you, m'boy." He clapped Ashtead on the shoulder. "My girl's told me of your intention to help, and I must say, I'm devilish glad to hear it. Wouldn't do for me to introduce her into my set. Though I must admit, I'm a bit surprised. I would have expected you to cut up stiff."

"So would I," Ashtead admitted. He glanced around. "Where's Lady Xanthe?"

"Amusing herself." Edwina's mouth tightened.

She fought back laughter, he realized with sudden unease. Yet try as he might, he could not conceive of the eminently respectable Lady Xanthe Simms behaving in any manner that would evoke such a reaction in Edwina.

His cousin slipped her hand through his arm. "There is a card room," she informed him. "Would you care for a hand, or would you prefer to introduce me to one of your friends?"

"Have you anyone in mind?" he asked dryly.

"I have heard of a Captain Kennilworth—"

Ashtead frowned. "I am barely acquainted with him, but I understand he rarely loses. I would recommend someone else."

"All right then." A dimple formed at the corner of her mouth. "Someone wealthy, and perhaps a trifle pompous. Do you know anyone suitable?"

Together they made their way to the adjoining chamber. He scanned the tables and spotted Lord Yardley, a heavyset gentleman fast approaching his fortieth year, who had inherited his barony at far too young an age. An air of consequence hovered about him that Ashtead had found irritating on more than one occasion. He drew Edwina in the man's general direction.

As he passed, he just brushed Yardley's elbow, then turned to him with an apologetic smile. "Beg your pardon, Yardley. Clumsy of me."

The man looked him up and down. "Ashtead. Well, can't be helped in your case, I suppose." He looked pointedly at Edwina.

"Allow me to present my cousin, Lady Edwina Langston. She was desirous of a game of piquet."

The baron rocked back on his heels. "So you play, my dear?" he asked in an irritatingly patronizing tone.

"My grandfather says I have become tolerable," she said meekly, her eyes downcast.

Yardley chuckled. "Well, old Shoreham used to know his cards, though I suppose age has taken its toll on him. Pity. Not many now who can give me sport."

Edwina raised her gaze to his face with a flattering

look of awe. "Oh, how I should adore the experience of playing against a truly excellent cardsman."

"Well, as to that, m'girl—" Yardley looked down his hawklike nose at her.

Ashtead gave an easy laugh. "No need to trouble him, Cousin Edwina. You'll find me just as challenging an opponent, I make no doubt."

Yardley stiffened. "You?" He snorted, dismissing Ashtead with a wave. He turned his attention fully on Edwina for the first time. "Come along, young lady. I'll show you how the game's played." He drew her off.

As Edwina turned away, she looked back at Ashtead over her shoulder, her eyes brimful of laughter. Minx, he reflected. He could only hope Edwina was as good as she believed. Yardley could use taking down a peg. Ashtead hovered near the table for the first rubber, which they played for reasonable stakes, and had the satisfaction of seeing Edwina taking trick after trick.

As they finished the hand, Yardley frowned, his gaze unfocused. "Another," he demanded. "You countered my obvious leads well enough, but there is much you can learn from me."

It would be Yardley who would learn, Ashtead wagered. He strolled away, leaving Eddie to handle the pompous oaf. He resigned himself to the dubious pleasure of listening to several young ladies performing ballads upon their hostess's pianoforte, all the while counting off half an hour. His gaze, he feared, strayed to the clock at far too frequent intervals. At last, as the hands crept toward his chosen time, he returned to the table where Lord Yardley and Edwina played the last few cards of their current hand. He strolled to the table as they tallied the difference in their score.

Yardley's eyes widened as he studied the total sum.

He cleared his throat. "Tolerably well, my dear, tolerably well. Still, you missed several of the more obvious of my intentional errors. But never mind. Perhaps I shall show you more another time."

"It would be a pleasure," Edwina assured him, her voice holding only the slightest touch of dryness.

"Of course." He inclined his head, accepting her words as the compliment he obviously felt to be his due. He drew a small wad of flimsies from his pocket and began to count them out. A surprising number of these he laid on the table before Edwina. "No," he said, although she had made no protest. "I insist. Permitting one's opponent to win is no excuse for a gentleman not to pay his debt of honor."

She accepted the bills, then looked up as Ashtead came to stand at her side. "Have you come to fetch me? We have just finished." She rose, thanked Yardley, and almost dragged Ashtead toward the door. "I do not believe I could have stood his company for another moment!" she breathed when they momentarily stood alone.

He looked down at her. "Regretting your choice of profession?"

"It is *not* a profession." She glared at him. "It is a temporary means to an end. And I knew when I began I must play with gentlemen who needed a sharp set down. But—"

"Doing can be very different from contemplating," he finished for her.

She looked up at him, her eyes large and wondering. "You understand."

His mouth twitched into a wry smile. "You don't have to sound so shocked."

"No." She resumed walking. "It is just that—"

"That after that night in your grandfather's room, you

believed me to be wholly without understanding or feeling?"

"Well—" She cast him a sideways look, and the muscles at the corners of her mouth tugged. "Yes."

He burst out laughing. "I see it is not only Yardley to whom you are giving set downs this night."

Soft color tinged her cheeks. "I beg your pardon."

"And so you should. Have you won sufficient for this evening, or do you desire me to introduce you to someone else?"

"I could not bear it tonight," she said.

"Then let us find your godmother, and you may set about enjoying yourself."

On the whole, he decided as he readied himself for bed that night, he had found it a very interesting evening. Edwina could be quite charming when she was not sticking barbs into his flesh. Her determination to win her independence at gaming he found fascinating. He ought to be shocked, he supposed, but he found himself too much in sympathy with her needs, even with the restrictions placed upon her because of her sex. No, he would help her, especially since that meant defying the old gentleman.

The following evening, he gratified his sister and aunt by offering to escort them to a musical *soiree*. Lydia stared at him and demanded to know what he was about.

"Brotherly duty," he assured her.

Lydia eyed him a moment longer, then looked to their Aunt Hester. "Has some new beauty arrived in Brighton?"

Aunt Hester seemed to subject this to some consideration. "One must have," she decided at last. "You may come, Ashtead, if you promise to make yourself useful and fetch lemonade for us at every interval."

Once arrived, he made a show of settling his sister and

aunt with various of their friends who were also in attendance, delivered the promised refreshments, then made good his escape. He strolled from room to room, greeting acquaintances, all the while searching for just one face. Had she gone elsewhere this night? he wondered as he completed his tour of the rooms. Perhaps she had feared there would be insufficient opportunity to pursue her intentions. Wherever she was, she would have trouble securing appropriate partners without his aid.

His smug satisfaction at her need for his assistance faded the next moment. Where the devil was she? He made his moody way to where Jacoby stood beside his sister's chair, deep in distracted thought. He looked his friend over, then turned to Lydia.

"He has had a new idea, and wished to work it through," she explained with amused tolerance. "What has brought you back so soon? Is your latest Incomparable not in attendance?"

He bit back the retort that it was only Edwina for whom he looked. He could never explain why, and Lydia would undoubtedly draw the wrong conclusions.

He was saved from the necessity of answering by the commencement of the first performance, by a young lady not quite far enough along with her harp lessons. When this at long last drew to a close, Ashtead excused himself to his Aunt Hester and slipped away. He'd spotted a card room—devoid of Edwina's presence—on his earlier tour, and that seemed a safe place to hide for the moment. But before he could seek refuge within, a stir at the front door announced a late arrival. He waited, and was rewarded with the sight of Lady Xanthe and Edwina.

So she had come. Did that mean no more lucrative venues offered themselves? Or did she indeed feel the need of the introductions he could provide? He watched while the ladies made their apologies to their hostess, then took seats to listen to the two gentlemen who tuned their violins for a duet. When at last this piece ended, Ashtead realized he had no notion what they had played. His thoughts had focused elsewhere. On Edwina.

She stood, paused beside Lydia to exchange greetings, spoke to Jacoby, who failed utterly to hear her, then strolled to where Ashtead leaned against the wall beside the door. Her eyebrows rose. "Have you no taste for music?" she asked. "You appear anxious to escape."

"Let us say curious to view the card room. I must confess to some interest in how you fare this night."

"Yes, I suppose you would. My independence ought to secure your fortune, should it not?"

He looked at her, frowning.

"Pray, do not pretend not to understand," she said. "Why else would you deign to help me? Once I have my independence, it will be obvious to my grandfather he cannot force me to do anything. There will then be no reason for him not to leave his fortune to you, so you may be easy." She swept ahead, entering the card room.

He caught up to her. "Is that what you really think?"

She looked up at him. "Well, of course. What else? Now." She looked about the sparsely populated apartment. "Do you see a likely partner for me?"

He wanted to remonstrate with her, explain that his motive in offering to introduce her t.o partners had been wholly altruistic. But he doubted she'd believe him. Well, she would come to recognize her error. Precisely how that would come about, he had not the least idea at the moment. So rather than dignify her assumption with a response, he turned his attention to the few gentlemen who already indulged in this more congenial pastime. Either of the two in the far corner would do for Edwina's purposes. He led her over to watch, performed the introduction when their game drew to a close, and within minutes Edwina accepted a place at the table. The displaced gentleman invited Ashtead to join him for a hand or two, and they found vacant chairs.

Steadfastly, he kept his gaze on his own cards, his attention on his own play. He had no need to glance at Edwina every few moments. Yet when he finally did succumb to the temptation nearly twenty minutes later, it was to find her playing with a different partner, the elderly Major Mickelby. She would come to no harm at his hands, nor could she put a serious dent into his seemingly bottomless purse. All in all, an excellent matching.

He returned to his own game, found he had played carelessly, and accepted his companion's laughing rebuke. He shuffled and dealt again, but Edwina's soft, melodic laugh caused him to falter. She certainly seemed to enjoy her chosen vocation. That annoyed him.

He took the first opportunity to confront her with her unseemly pleasure in her equally unseemly occupation.

"It is no such thing!" she declared, keeping her voice pitched low to avoid attracting attention. "Would you rather I allowed myself to be forced into marrying you? Positioned as I am, the choice seems to be between that, or starving, or the course I have chosen to follow. I am not about to let my preferences interfere with what I must accomplish."

With that, she pushed past him, leaving him staring after her. Another damsel, he reflected, might well have yielded to the pressures brought to bear on her. Another might have lost her nerve and proved unable to carry out so outrageous a plan. But not Edwina. He had to admire her courage. At least he would, if he did not find her spirit and outspokenness so damnably annoying.

Six

Eddie bade her hostess good night, then followed Xanthe and Ashtead to the door. Another card party, another evening of quiet winning, of amused surprise on the part of her partners. She'd pursued this pastime for the better part of two weeks now, and a tidy little sum lay hidden in her room. In her reticule she could feel the comfortable weight of just over 280 pounds more. She'd followed her own rules too, never winning much from any one person, and allowing at least a week to pass before she played again with any of her opponents.

She descended the shallow steps to the Steyne. She could hear the muted roar of the ocean as the waves rushed in to wash the sand, then pulled back to briefly join the eddying waters before the next wave crashed forward. It was a beautiful evening, still warm but with a cool, salt-tinged breeze blowing off the sea. A sliver of moon, rapidly fading to new, glimmered on the swells. She was glad they had elected to walk the few hundred yards along the Marine Parade to their house.

Xanthe crossed the road to stroll beside the sand. Not that she'd get any on her slippers. The little fairy hummed softly, and the soles of her satin shoes skimmed a clear inch in the air. Edwina glanced quickly at Ashtead, but he seemed oblivious to the fairy's magical activities. He gazed toward the water, pacing in silence at her side.

Xanthe drifted ahead, and a lilting melody filled Eddie's mind. Tiny fairies, no bigger than butterflies, flitted through the air, tugging at Xanthe's sleeves, perching amid her looping braids. Miniature winged cats joined their carefree dance; then a little horse dipped and swirled among the other flying creatures. Then an ostrich, a lion, even an ungainly elephant with gossamer wings joined the acrobatic troupe. Eddie caught her lower lip between her teeth to keep from laughing.

"You seem happy," Ashtead said.

She looked up to see him smiling down at her. He walked closer to her than she had realized; if she moved only slightly, her shoulder would brush his arm. She eased a step away. "I have never been more so in my entire life."

"Your first taste of society and parties?" he hazarded.

She turned to look fully at him. "My first taste of freedom."

He stared back, his expression unreadable in the pale light of the midnight sky.

She slowed her steps, searching for words to explain. "For the first time, I am able to make my own decisions, choose how I shall spend the day or evening, purchase what I like, and with my own money. I do not believe I could ever tolerate someone controlling me again. This brief taste of—oh, of being *myself*, has confirmed my intentions never to enter into a marriage of convenience." Which thought raised certain grievances she had thrust to the back of her mind. The new easiness between them emboldened her to drag them forth. "How you could ever have insulted me by agreeing to marry me for my grandfather's money—"

He held up a hand, interrupting her. "That is ancient history. And I might add I never would have done so had I not been so furious—and so drunk."

Indignation vied with amusement over the implied insult, and evaporated. A soft laugh escaped her. "You are most complimentary, my lord. And you may be certain I shall never place any other gentleman in so uncomfortable a position. I shall find a quiet village—by the seaside, I believe." She fell silent as her imagination constructed an idealized little grouping of shops and cottages, each with a kitchen garden and perhaps a cow for milk and cheese, some hens for eggs—

"You would live alone?" He sounded curious, perhaps a touch irritated.

"No." She fought back her regret. "That would not be at all the thing. Just because I desire to be independent does not mean I intend to cast off all the constraints of society. I shall find some impoverished female relation to share it with me, to lend me countenance. Someone meek and biddable, of course, who shall not try to tyrannize over me."

"It sounds a bore."

She raised her eyebrows. "What, a future of peace untrammeled by masculine decrees and managing? To me it sounds like heaven."

"If you find masculine company so repellent, I shall relieve you of my presence." With a curt good night, he strode quickly ahead, on to the house where he stayed with his aunt.

Eddie watched the rigid set of his back, not certain whether to be amused or sorry. She had offended him with her views; he had made that obvious enough. Yet whatever he might think, it had not been her intention to do so. She'd been happy, relaxed, talking of her dreams.

She tried to thrust his irritation from her mind, yet it wouldn't budge. It was, she admitted at last, a bit of a puzzle. Fortunes aside, he wished to marry her as little as she wished to marry him. So why should her stated determination not to become leg-shackled annoy him? Unless he still, and despite his assurances to the contrary, coveted marriage to her as a sure path to her grandfather's fortune. Disappointment flooded through her, lowering her spirits, destroying her contentment of just moments before.

When she gained her competence, she would move far away. Very far away. And then she would never have to see him again.

Yet even reaching that decision could not ease her sudden restlessness. She slept fitfully, rose as soon as it was light, and let herself out of the house to pace along the lonely shore. Only it wasn't lonely, not even at this early hour. The bathing machine attendants manned their posts, and already they enjoyed a few customers. Three of the contraptions stood wheel-high in the lapping waters, their horses standing peacefully, heads lowered as if they dozed with the sun warming their backs and the water cooling their legs.

As Eddie watched, the door to one of the boxes opened, and two women attendants sprang forward to assist a middle-aged matron down the ladder. As her foot entered the swelling waters, a cry escaped the matron, but she persevered, descending the submerged steps. Her white shift billowed out, then clung to her as she stepped to the ocean floor and waded, waist deep, on the arms of her two dippers.

Cold, Eddie reflected, but definitely refreshing. It

might even restore one's flagging spirits. She strolled forward, watching the stately tred of an elderly gentleman who seemed to be enjoying his outing. Only one attendant hovered at his side; he probably indulged in this pastime on a regular basis.

"Care to enter the waters, miss?" called a deep, female voice from nearby.

Eddie turned to regard the stout woman. A kindly face, a respectable, capable appearance, a no-nonsense manner— "Yes," Eddie declared, surprising herself. She picked her way across the sand to stroke the Roman nose of the restful bay gelding harnessed to the bathing machine, then moved around the back to climb the ladder leading up to the box. The attendant supplied her with a muslin shift and cap, and helped her unfasten her gown.

A man's voice, at very close range, said, "Step easy, there, Samuel. Back now. Back. Good fellow."

The cart trembled, then rolled over the harder, damp sand. Eddie caught her balance on the wooden wall, then finished changing. The attendant hung her gown and undergarments from a peg, placed her slippers on a shelf, then opened the door and descended the ladder. Eddie stood at the top, staring down at the waters swirling about the cart's wheels, flowing toward the shore, then out once more, only to be turned by a new flood of incoming wavelets. Delight welled in her at this sensation of freedom, and she descended the ladder. Then her toes touched the chill of the sea. An exclamation, half a laugh, half a protest, escaped her; then she recklessly jumped free, splashing into the ocean, shivering as the cold enveloped her to just above her waist.

"Easy there, miss." The attendant grasped her arm in

a firm hold. "Now, walking will feel odd, so you just move slowly."

Eddie took a tentative step, then another, then impulsively leaned back, allowing the buoyancy of the water to support her weight. Beside her the wavelets broke into a roiling, bubbling mass. Alarmed, she pulled away.

"Easy, miss," the attendant said, as calm as ever.

Eddie stared at her, then at the disturbed waters in which she could now clearly see a miniature ship being tossed. Xanthe, of course. Eddie lay back in the cradling swells, ready to enjoy whatever her fairy godmother offered.

A serpent's head broke the surface, a comical face with tufted ears, pointed snout, and whirling eyes the deep violet of Xanthe's. His long, sinuous body swirled through the depths. Then one claw emerged from the foam, a delicate china teacup and saucer clasped daintily. He grinned, revealing multiple rows of gleaming white fangs; then he popped down to the depths and vanished.

A moment later a golden fish emerged in his place, swimming at speed, a long trailer of seaweed clamped in its mouth. Xanthe, standing upon two flat sticks of wood, held the other end as the fish pulled her across the ocean's surface. Three dolphins rose next, lifting their sleek bodies above the surface until only their tails remained hidden. They hovered in this untenable position, then shot backward, still upright, until they vanished into the distance. Two more appeared, leaping into the air in an aquatic ballet.

Eddie, delighted, shot a glance at her attendant, but the poor woman remained oblivious to Xanthe's efforts. It seemed a shame that not everyone could share in the wonder and joy of the fairy's magic. Even as Eddie watched, the attendant's form blurred, her body from the waist down growing scales, her legs transforming into a tail. Beside Eddie now swam a mermaid with a wreath of water lilies in hair that flowed rather than being confined beneath a cap. Other mermaids joined the first, miming swimming strokes until Eddie joined in their play.

"Careful now, miss," cried the one who stood closest to her.

A gentle hand caught Eddie's elbow. For a moment the magic faded, and the prosaic, dependable attendant once more stood at her side. Then bubbles roiled about her, and Eddie found herself facing a mustachioed walrus regarding her through a quizzing glass.

Ashtead strode along the Steyne, restless, his gaze scanning the throng of Fashionables who took part in the morning promenade. He nodded to a number of acquaintances, but found he had no desire to stop to speak to any of them. This was no idle walk, he realized with growing irritation. He had come for only one purpose, more fool he. He searched the throng for one face, for one gracefully moving figure. And he couldn't see her anywhere.

A lilting melody filled his mind, and he found he hummed along with it. Abruptly he turned and paced back down the street to the beach. He scanned it, noting several people walking by the water's edge. Two nurserymaids sat on a blanket in close conversation while their several charges excavated in the sand. Farther along, fishermen had drawn their dories up beyond the tide line; the gulls swept low with their mournful cries, trying to snatch tidbits of fish cast aside by the men who cleaned their catch. Several cats prowled the area, ducking from the attacking birds, making off with their fair share of the morning's haul.

He continued across the soft sand, toward the bathing machines with their horses and attendants. Several brave souls had even ventured into the sea, he noted with amused admiration for their adventurous spirits. One matron paraded slowly back and forth, never more than two yards from her ladder. An elderly gentleman walked determinedly, venturing far afield under the watchful guidance of two husky young men. A frail gentleman stood still, one dipper holding each of his arms as he stared, shivering, down into the waters. And a young lady swam with tentative strokes and splashed playfully at something he could not see.

He slowed, his gaze following the girl's figure, to which her shift clung in a most revealing and agreeable manner. A gull shrilled out its cry, circling low about him, regarding him with the hopeful eye of a bird in search of stray crusts. Ashtead moved on, his gaze lingering appreciatively on the young lady.

She turned to face him, stared a moment, then waved. Either a remarkably brazen young miss, or— He peered at her, and with a sense of shock recognized her as Edwina.

His surprise wavered into displeasure. Lord, had the chit no more sense than to display her charms for any rakehell's ogling? He would have to warn her. Except to do so, he would have to admit to having seen a great deal of her charms himself. And she possessed a great many of them, worthy of considerable admiration. That took him aback. Little Edwina had blossomed indeed.

With a word to the woman at her side, Edwina swam back to the wheeled box and scrambled up the ladder. The man holding the horse led the animal slowly from the shallow wavelets, back to the shore, drawing the box with them. Several minutes passed. Then Edwina sprang lightly down, thanked her attendants, and ran across the sand to join Ashtead. Pleasure flushed her face, her hair hung in tight, wet ringlets about her face, and he had never seen her look so lovely.

"I must go inside at once," she exclaimed. "I could not bear to draw on my stockings because of the sand. Are you returning home, or were you just going out?"

At the moment, he couldn't remember. He simply stared at her as rational thought was blotted out by awareness of her, of the laughter and energy that filled her. She was much more than just his second cousin, much more than her grandfather's heiress. He could never recall seeing a young lady so lovely, so very much what he needed in his life.

She tilted her head to one side. "Are you all right? You look a little odd."

"Yes." With an effort, he kept his gaze from lowering from her face, from further exploring those discoveries he had just made. Yet as prudent as it might be, he could not bring himself to leave her. "I was about to pay a morning call on your godmother," he extemporized.

She led the way to the house, where she left him in the care of their majordomo while she made her way up the stairs. The man admitted him to the salon, where he found Lady Xanthe sipping tea. The massive cat Titus lolled on a pier table, his vast expanse of stomach turned to the rays that streamed through the lace curtain. The feline blinked sleepy eyes in his direction, then returned to the all-important business of sunning himself.

Lady Xanthe smiled her serene smile, hummed a soft measure to herself, and amusement crinkled the corners of her eyes. He always experienced the sensation that she enjoyed some joke of which he wasn't aware, but it didn't bother him. He sensed no malice in her.

She set down her cup. "Thank you for escorting dear Eddie home." Her soft, musical voice hinted at laughter.

"I was tempted to join her," he admitted.

A footman entered, bearing a tray on which rested a tankard of ale. He took a sip and found it a remarkably fine brew. Better, in fact, than he could ever remember tasting. He took another swallow, his appreciation growing.

"Do have a cake." Xanthe gestured toward a heavily laden platter.

He didn't remember seeing the plate before, but the thick slices, filled with nuts and smelling deliciously of cinnamon, proved too tempting to ignore. He was finishing his third when Edwina swept into the room, her long hair a mass of damp curls caught by a riband at the nape of her neck. She looked absurdly young, and even more desirable than he remembered.

"Will you be attending the concert on the Pavilion grounds this afternoon?" he asked abruptly. "I had thought to make up a party, for my sister and aunt have mentioned how much they would enjoy it."

"It would be delightful," Xanthe declared, "but I fear we have other plans. I feel certain you will enjoy it, though."

Ashtead did not feel so sure. He could count on Jacoby to occupy Lydia, he supposed. He might be able to convince Colonel Chesterfield to keep Aunt Hester company, but that would leave him no one with whom to talk. It didn't help any that his sole interest in the event would have been to watch Edwina's pleasure. Irritated, both with the ladies for not coming and with himself for having suggested the idea in the first place, he took his leave, announcing he had people to find and invitations to issue.

He encountered Jacoby almost as soon as he turned onto the Steyne. His friend blinked vaguely at him, and when Ashtead had repeated the proposal only three times, Jacoby professed himself delighted with the plan, and even offered to pay a call in the Marine Parade to inform Mrs. Winslow and Lydia of the proffered treat. That left Ashtead to begin his search for Colonel Chesterfield, but a tour of Donaldson's produced not that gentleman but Mr. Marmaduke Rutland, who eyed him shrewdly when he suggested the scheme.

"Some matron you need squired, m'boy?" the old gamester demanded.

Ashtead fought back a smile at this directness. "Just so. My aunt."

"Ah." Marmaduke considered. "Then you'll want me on my best behavior, I'll wager. Never fear, dear boy, never fear. I know how to do the pretty when it's required of me."

He did, it seemed. Ashtead, seated between the two couples, had the dubious pleasure of observing his aunt's amused enjoyment as the old rascal proceeded to captivate her. If Ashtead were not careful, he would find the old roué a regular guest at their dinner table.

Matters proceeded upon a different line on his other side. Jacoby engaged Lydia in earnest conversation, but its sole purpose seemed to be the discovery of dramatic possibilities for the child he had introduced into his play. Twice he interrupted Lydia to jot down some idea that had just occurred to him, leaving her to address the remainder of her remark to the side of his head.

Well, what did she expect? Ashtead mused, watching the indulgent look in her eyes begin to fade. The first time she met Jacoby, he'd been consumed by his work. Only a peagoose would expect his personality to alter. And only another peagoose would be taken in by Mr. Marmaduke Rutland, he added to himself as his aunt's delighted laugh sounded. Really, females were a breed apart and not to be fathomed by mere males.

When the concert ended, they strolled through the gardens, Aunt Hester on Marmaduke's arm, her head tilted upward to hear whatever outrageous comment he currently made. Lydia paced beside Jacoby, the latter once more far away in a world of his own creation, oblivious to all that surrounded him. And what the devil was Edwina about this afternoon that she could not have come to enliven the outing for him? Ashtead seethed as he followed the others.

He was saved from the prospect of an evening spent in the unsatisfactory company of his female relatives by an encounter with Colonel Chesterfield, which resulted in an invitation to a card party after dinner at that gentleman's lodgings. "High stakes, an excellent burgundy, an even better claret, and no females," the colonel assured him, which exactly suited Ashtead's mood.

In fact, an evening spent alternately drinking to Edwina's eyes and damning them ended up suiting him all too well. For what possible purpose other than aggravation did men need women anyway? The muzzy thought ran through his head. Then visions of Edwina would once more fill his mind, of her slender body and full curves revealed by that wet shift, of the laughter in her eyes, of the determined tilt of her chin. Then he'd mutter an oath under his breath, drain his current glass of wine, and lay down a reckless card. Before the party drew to a close, he had broached his fourth bottle.

As the others rose to take their leave in the early

hours of the morning, he remained sprawled in his chair, moodily staring at the dregs of the deep ruby liquid that lingered in his cup. It had occurred to him he was no longer in possession of any feet. Yet when he stared at his pantaloons long enough to bring them into focus, he could follow their course down to his stockings, then farther to the shoes that were undeniably his own, and equally undeniably filled.

Just how he returned to his aunt's house, he had no clear recollection. Nor did he make any serious attempt at remembering when, some hours later, he stirred at last in his own bed. His head ached abominably, his mouth felt as if he had eaten his unwashed stockings, and the aromas of kippered herrings and cinnamon buns that rose from the lower floors left him queasy.

He groped one arm out from beneath the covers and held out his hand. Barely a moment passed before he felt a glass pressed into it. Good old experienced Ottley. He tried to guide the remedy to his mouth, found firm hands pressed over his, and shortly swallowed his valet's personal receipt.

He lay back with a groan and waited. An unpleasant minute passed; then his eyeballs imploded and his stomach convulsed. He lay still for a minute longer, then opened bleary eyes. "Thank you," he managed to gasp.

"You are quite welcome, my lord." Ottley recovered the cup. "It has been some weeks since my little restorative has been needed." The man set quietly to the task of laying out a fresh shirt and neckcloth, and within a surprisingly short time, the valet was able to send Ashtead downstairs to face a breakfast of a rare beefsteak and a tankard of ale.

Lydia glided into the breakfast parlor a short time later, in search of her nuncheon. She pulled up short at sight of him, looked him over, and shook her head. "Men," she pronounced scathingly. "How can it possibly afford you any pleasure to face the day in a state like this?"

He regarded her through eyes still bleary. She wore a sunny gown of jonquil muslin and a chip-straw bonnet adorned with matching ribands. He winced. "Must you shout so, Lydia?"

"Must you drink so, Ashtead?" she countered in a fair mimicry of his pained tone. "You are to escort us to the ball at the Old Ship this night. Pray do not forget."

The ball. Memory flooded back. There would be a card room, and he had secured several agreeable partners for Edwina during the course of the previous evening. At least, he thought he had. His memory had yet to return. Still, the day seemed brighter.

He declined his sister's invitation to escort her to Donaldson's Lending Library, and instead strolled along the beach, breathing deeply of the cleansing air, his gaze searching the waters surrounding the bathing machines. Yet not so much as a glimpse did he catch of the one person he wanted to see. If Edwina had indulged herself again, she must have done so at an earlier hour. Irritated, he made his way to the Old Ship, where he had left his cattle and curricle, for his grays must be as badly in need of exercise as he. He would have preferred to ride, but tooling his pair about the countryside was better than nothing. He returned in a much better mood.

For once, he arrived in the salon before the two ladies descended the stairs for dinner. This won a comment of surprised approval from Aunt Hester. She went to him, kissed his cheek, and called him a dear, good boy.

Lydia, entering moments later, looked him over with critical appraisal from the doorway. "Elegant," she ad-

mitted at last. "Are you out to ensnare some poor female?"

"Try not to be more of a fool than you can help," he
advised her, and escorted them in to the excellent dinner
that awaited them.

He delivered his party to the inn less than twenty minutes after the appointed time for the ball to begin. Already the rooms were comfortably filled, but though he
strolled about with Aunt Hester on his arm, he could
see no sign of Edwina. Looking for her was becoming
a habit with him, he realized, and was not pleased by
that fact.

But when she arrived a few minutes later, his irritation
evaporated. He made no move toward her, though he
noted several gentlemen approach her obtaining dances.
And no wonder they flocked to her. She had blossomed
into a beauty, possessed of both elegance and poise. He
had better secure a dance with her himself, for he had
not the least doubt she would refuse him if her filling
card offered her the least excuse.

As he expected, Edwina sighed and shook her head
when he asked if she had a waltz free. "I am engaged
for far too many dances," she informed him in a near-
whisper. "I will hardly have time to visit the card room."

The earnestness of her tone made him smile. "I have
found two new partners for you." He watched with appreciation as her large eyes brightened. "For the price
of that waltz."

A laugh burst from her, a lovely sound, fresh and real.
"Very well then. I can only hope their ability makes the
sacrifice worthwhile."

A young, nondescript gentleman claimed her for the
set that formed, and she moved away on her gallant's
arm. Ashtead's gaze lingered on her retreating figure;

then he pulled himself out of his reverie. He had no desire to make a cake of himself by simply standing there watching her. He solicited the hand of an old acquaintance, Miss Augusta Talbridge, whose late arrival meant she had not yet bestowed her hand for the coming country dance.

To his satisfaction, she proved more than willing to flirt with him. She was quite a beauty, a regular diamond of the first water, and he indulged her, whispering teasing compliments into her ear whenever the movements of the dance brought them close. He did not bring a blush to her cheeks, though; this was a young lady expert in the art of dalliance. When the final notes faded at last, he turned her over to one of her many admirers, then sought out the ambitious Miss Fanny Marlowe, whisking her away from under the noses of three young gentlemen of impoverished means but handsome countenances.

And next would come his waltz with Edwina. He found his thoughts leaping ahead, with the result that his normally elegant toe suffered a trifle. Miss Marlowe uttered a teasing rebuke, but the reproof in her eyes made it clear she expected more from her partner than a wandering mind. He apologized, concentrating very hard on Miss Marlowe for the next several minutes; then his thoughts drifted once more to the anticipated delights of the waltz.

As soon as he returned her to her waiting court, he sought out Edwina. She had also just left the floor, and her face glowed with pleasure. Lydia joined her, dismissing both their previous partners with a smile and gesture of her hand. She leaned close to Edwina and said something that brought a choke of laughter from the girl.

His sister looked up as he approached. "What, have you run out of beauties? He is the most shocking flirt, you must know," she added to Edwina.

Edwina allowed her gaze to rest on him for no more than a moment. In a voice of complete indifference, she said, "Oh, I can readily believe that. He has demonstrated it quite adequately this night."

"Be glad you have forsworn all gentlemen, my dear cousin." With a mischievous smile for her brother, Lydia strolled off to meet her next partner.

Ashtead watched her departure with exasperation. "I see my sister is in her usual funning humor. I suppose she has been cataloging my faults for you?"

"Oh, I doubt she'd have time," came the airy response.

That took him aback. He thought Edwina had come to regard him as an ally, someone with whom she could exchange a friendly word. Her antagonism left him off balance. What, he wondered, could Lydia have said? Thrusting his irritation with his sister aside, he led the way to the floor, where they took up their positions as the musicians played the opening bars. Edwina took his hand, turning from him in the opening steps, looking about the room rather than at him.

He had never known anyone quite like her. Not just her independent nature, her determination to make her own way in life, which he alternately enjoyed and deplored. Everything about her fascinated him. She moved with a grace that commanded the eye, her steps light and flowing, so that he found pleasure in simply gazing at her. Her cheeks flushed softly with the exercise, lending color to an already lovely countenance.

He drew her near, his arm encircling her slender waist for the closed turn; then she moved away again, out of his grasp. He resisted the impulse to pull her back; she would return in just a few short measures. As she stepped toward him once more, his hand clasped her waist, his arm encircling her, tightening about her. The top of her curls tickled his nose; the scent of violets and roses clung to her hair. He inhaled deeply, then stood still as required by the dance, allowing her to cross behind him, holding his right hand in hers as she reached for his left to begin the slow, pivoting turn.

Sensation flooded through him, awareness of her touch, her scent, her nearness. Memory flickered in his mind of her playing in the water, of the drenched shift clinging to her curves. She'd seemed a water nymph, all laughter and light. And now— Now she was a fairy princess, delicate and graceful, and so very warm in his arms. They ached to hold her, to draw her closer than propriety would ever permit. He wanted to breathe her in, taste her tantalizing lips. He could easily fall in love with her.

Love. That was a new concept for him. What he felt when he thought of Edwina had nothing to do with the casual but enjoyable liaisons he had formed over the years, nothing to do with the delightful flirtations with other young ladies of quality.

He continued through the movements of the dance, waiting for those few moments when he could draw her close once more. She felt right in his arms, as if she belonged there. Yes, he could very easily come to love her.

If he hadn't already.

His heart twisted with yearning, only to plummet the next moment. He could never convince her he wanted her for her own sake, for her laughter and love, for her spirit, for the way she looked up at him through her lashes and made his heart melt. Whatever he did, however he paid her court, she would always believe he wanted her grandfather's fortune.

Seven

The actors withdrew from the stage for the interval, but Eddie remained where she sat at the front of the box, leaning forward, eyes wide. Even after the last costumed man disappeared from view, she remained there, not wanting to relinquish the magic. At last a sigh escaped her, and she sat back in her chair.

"A paltry affair," pronounced Lydia as she settled in the seat at Eddie's side. "They quite deserved to have the audience booing and throwing things at them."

"Oh, no." Eddie shook her head. "It was wonderful."

Lydia stared at her, incredulous. "You cannot say you enjoyed the melodrama!"

"Indeed I did! I have never seen anything like it before."

"She has never before visited a theater." Ashtead drew a chair forward, seating himself just behind them.

Eddie turned, reaching out to lay her hand on his sleeve. "It was so very kind of you to hire this box for us. I shall never forget this treat."

"Oh, if it is your first visit," Lydia declared, "then I daresay you would enjoy anything."

"Must be the company," pronounced Mr. George Elliston, an amiable young gentleman selected by Ashtead to bear Lydia company. Jacoby, who would normally have filled that role, had flatly refused to view any dramatic productions while he worked on his own.

Lydia threw a flirtatious look at Elliston over her shoulder. "Indeed the company has been quite delightful."

Xanthe, who had sat in one corner of the box engaged in lively conversation with Colonel Chesterfield, looked up. "In all, a most agreeable time. Did you not find it so, Mrs. Winslow?"

Mrs. Winslow turned from her low-voiced conversation with Marmaduke Rutland. "Most diverting," she agreed.

Mr. Elliston beamed at Lydia. "Care to go for a stroll? Plenty of time before the next act."

"How thoughtful of you." Lydia rose and accepted his arm, and the two of them left the box.

Eddie watched the departure with a slight frown. She could not help but be aware of the flirtation the two had conducted since their arrival at the theater, and it puzzled her. She had no fault to find with Mr. Elliston, except perhaps that his intellect was not profound. Yet he did not seem the type to fascinate Lydia. Perhaps she did not know Ashtead's sister as well as she thought.

She became aware that her hand still rested on Ashtead's arm. She tried to withdraw it, but he caught her fingers and raised them fleetingly to his lips before releasing them. Warm color flooded her cheeks, and she looked back to the stage. "There will be a pantomime next?" she inquired, more for something to say than any need to know. She had studied the program with enthusiasm when they had first arrived.

He drew his chair closer. "Have you forgiven me for keeping you from the gaming tables this night?"

"Readily." And she found she meant it. She looked

away, back to the stage, where workmen dragged various props and scenery for the next entertainment. "I am doing very well. At this moment, I could purchase a small cottage, though I have not yet enough to support myself and a companion. And I know I have you to thank for much of my success." She looked down, suddenly shy. "I am very grateful for the introductions to suitable gentlemen."

"And they are not done yet." A jocular note entered his voice as he made light of his efforts on her behalf. "This afternoon I encountered George Yarborough. He is just the thing, a shrewd player with few scruples. I should very much enjoy seeing him suffer a rousing defeat at the hands of a female."

"Losing will not prove a hardship on him?" she asked quickly.

"Only upon his conceit, which will do him a vast amount of good. You may have the dubious pleasure of making his acquaintance tomorrow night."

A delighted laugh sounded from the back of the box, and Eddie turned to see Mrs. Winslow and her Uncle Marmaduke convulsed in mirth. The glowing look her reprobate relative bestowed upon his companion startled Eddie. Had she been so involved in her own worries she had failed to notice what went on about her, what concerned her beloved relative so nearly?

And if only some gentleman might one day gaze at her like that, with admiration touched with something more, something almost predatory and altogether exciting. If Ashtead looked at her with that devastating combination—She broke off that thought, breathless at the mere prospect, and confused she should react in that manner.

When had her sentiments undergone so dramatic a

change? She had despised him, sought his company only as an expediency. And now— She lowered her gaze to her hands, then turned to the stage, where the first of the actors strode into position. Once, in her first, brief, glimpse of him as he'd arrived at the Castle, she had indulged in a romantic daydream centered about his dashing, elegant figure. But that had been before she had known what hateful purpose had brought him. Her dream had died abruptly when he had fallen in a drunken stupor at her feet. But now that she was better acquainted with him, understood his temper—

She risked a sideways glance at him, and found he watched her. He smiled, his expression warm, intimate, and her heart beat faster. With an effort, she remembered to breathe.

But she was being a fool. Friendliness she could allow, but nothing more. She slid toward the front of her chair, away from him. He set out to captivate her on purpose, she reminded herself. It wasn't she that he courted, but her grandfather's fortune. She could not let herself forget that, not for a single moment.

Lydia and Elliston returned, still carrying on their flirtation. They reclaimed their chairs, and their voices dropped to whispers as the last of the actors took his place. Eddie listened to the pair's lighthearted banter, and wished she could treat Ashtead with such ease.

Sleep did not come easily that night, nor did it linger. Dreams of Ashtead's singularly appealing smile alternated with bouts of wakefulness, during which times she reminded herself of his iniquities, and upbraided herself for falling under his spell. Marriage to him—to any man—was the last thing she wanted. So why must thoughts of him haunt her?

She rose late, heavy-eyed, and descended to the breakfast table. Two chafing dishes rested on the sideboard, with Titus sprawled between them. "Hoping for a treat?" she inquired, and lifted the lid of the first.

Inside rested not the coddled eggs she had expected, but a miniature cottage, complete with rambling roses and ivy. She stared at it for a long moment, then replaced the lid and picked up the other. Inside, small bands of gold swam in a cream sauce.

"Most amusing," she said, her voice flat.

Titus merely blinked at her.

"Xanthe?" She looked about, but though she could hear soft humming, the fairy was nowhere in sight.

"Choices," the fairy's soft voice seemed to breathe in her ear.

Eddie shook her head. "I've made my choice. I don't want to be controlled by anyone!"

"Did your father control your mother?"

The rings in the dish lost shape, swirled, transformed. In their place she glimpsed her mother's face, smiling with a tenderness that made her heart ache. "No," she whispered. "But Ashtead—"

"You don't truly know him. And he likes to be controlled as little as do you." The image rippled, faded, and in its place lay prosaic slices of ham.

Titus emitted a staccato sound.

Eddie shook her head and served herself.

The sunshine beckoned her outdoors, and as she strolled across the sand toward the water, a cloud of gossamer strands descended slowly from the sky to hover before her. With a flutter of her rounded wings, Xanthe stepped from it. The mists swirled about her fairy form, then turned into a flock of gulls that swooped back toward the sky. Feathers—not all of them avian—fluttered to the sand.

"Original," said Eddie.

Xanthe beamed at her. "One should always look for the little delights in life."

"But not all of us can make our own," Eddie countered.

Xanthe shook her head. "Indeed you can. It is all in how you look at things. There is magic everywhere. But most people don't let themselves see it." With that, the fairy vanished, only to reappear moments later beside a small family group near the water's edge.

Lydia, Eddie realized, along with her two children and their nursemaid. She did not see Ashtead with them. Not sure whether she was disappointed or glad, Eddie strolled over to join them. Already, Xanthe knelt in the sand beside little Anne and little Lord Harcourt, busily constructing a castle. With considerable magical aid, Eddie guessed, admiring the creation that took rapid and glorious form.

She returned Lydia's greeting, then settled on the blanket at her friend's side. Sun warmed her skin, and the cool sea breeze ruffled her hair. A tang of salt filled her lungs. Perhaps Xanthe was right. Perhaps she didn't need the fairy's magical humming to find a measure of true delight.

Lydia looked up from her contemplation of the sea, still smiling, but her expression faded to a frown as her gaze passed beyond Eddie. "Here is Sir William. I wonder whether he will emerge sufficiently from his dramatic endeavors to notice us."

Eddie turned to see Jacoby picking his careful way across the soft sand. He looked as if he had slept in his pantaloons and shirt, merely shrugging himself into his unbrushed coat and dragging on his unpolished Hessians before taking himself out of doors. His hair, his sole unmussable attribute, gleamed in the morning light.

"Good morning!" Eddie called as he passed less than ten yards away without appearing to notice them. He kept walking without so much as a glance in their direction.

Lydia sighed. "It is useless, Eddie. When he is involved in his work, he disdains even the most basic of civilities."

"I do not think it is that, precisely." Eddie watched his retreating figure. "It is just that he is oblivious to everything and everyone else."

"Which is no better," Lydia declared. "Something ought to be done about that man. I shall speak to Ashtead about him."

Some half hour later, Jacoby strode back up the beach. This time, far from walking right past them, he stopped and sketched them a bow. The distracted look had vanished from his face, which beamed now with pleasure.

Eddie shaded her eyes against the sun as she looked up at him. "You have worked out your current problem?"

"Only if he has hired a valet," murmured Lydia.

"A very great problem," Jacoby assured Eddie. He showed no sign of having heard Lydia's interjection. "I must return to my rooms to write down my ideas before they quite desert me. You must excuse me." With that, he directed a nod toward them both and strode off.

"Impossible man. I cannot think why I worry about him, except that he is Ashtead's friend." Lydia rose. "It is time I took the children home."

She minced her way across the sand to where Xanthe still worked on her sand castle. The fairy had created an impressive structure; its turrets rose high, its battlements wide. Little Anne dug a mote around its base. At once this filled with water, and another tower joined its fellows. Tiny multicolored flags fluttered in the breeze. A miniature dragon, glittering amethyst and ruby, swooped down from the sky, blowing fire at the tiny armored knights who charged to attack the sandy fortress. Anne squealed in delight, and infant Gregory stared wide-eyed. Apparently, the children could see Xanthe's workings.

"It is time to go," Lydia said.

Anne cried out in protest, and little Lord Harcourt raised wide eyes first to his sister, then to his mother. After a moment, he returned his full attention to the pile of sand he patted into an ever larger hill.

"I will bring them back safe in a little while, if you wish to go now," Xanthe said. She hummed a slow, stately bar.

Lydia nodded without smiling. "It is very kind of you, dear Lady Xanthe. I—I find I have the headache." With that, she turned to make her way across the beach as quickly as the soft sand would allow.

Eddie watched her retreat with a frown. Poor Lydia. That Jacoby fascinated her friend, she could not doubt. That Lydia also found him frustrating and unsatisfactory in many ways was also obvious. But why did the man trouble Lydia so greatly? The young woman should be eager to avoid any emotional entanglements; after all, she'd endured a marriage that had shattered her romantic hopes. And why, Eddie reflected, should she herself even contemplate for so much as a moment entering that hallowed but frequently unhappy state of wedlock? It defied all reason.

With an effort, she thrust these unproductive thoughts

aside. She needed to win a competence, and that meant concentrating on her cards, not allowing herself to be distracted by a pair of troublesome gentlemen.

That evening, she attended the Bradleighs' *soiree,* and soon found her way to the card room. In a very short time, Uncle Marmaduke joined her there, standing at her side, watching, nodding his approval of her every move. Just having him there gave her a measure of much-needed confidence.

But he wasn't the only one who watched her, Eddie realized with a sudden tinge of uneasiness. Several other young gentlemen, not of the highest *ton,* stood nearby, their attention focused on her play. She tried to ignore them, to focus on the all-important task of winning, but their presence lingered in her awareness.

As the next hand drew to a close, Uncle Marmaduke leaned forward, just touching her shoulder. "Sorry, m'dear. Must steal you away, for your godmamma will be wondering where you are."

"My godmamma knows perfectly well where I am," Eddie whispered to her disreputable relative as he drew her from the card room.

Marmaduke nodded. "Diversion," he explained. "You saw those bucks standing just to one side? Betting on you to win."

She stopped, staring at him in dismay. "Betting? On me?"

He took her arm. "Now, no real harm done, but we don't want your name to become a byword, m'dear."

"No," she agreed with feeling.

"Tell you what." He patted her hand. "Don't you play for a day or two. Say it's begun to bore you. Let the gossip settle."

With that plan, she could only acquiesce. She had won

a great deal; she could afford to take several nights off. Then she could begin again, with a suitable show of reluctance.

The following evening put her resolve to the test. They attended a *soiree* given by the dowager Lady Gresham, and within minutes of their arrival, Ashtead brought George Yarborough to present to her. This rather dandified young gentleman, with an air of consequence and a nose designed for looking down upon the world, expressed his rather bored intention to honor Eddie with a game of cards. Eddie knew serious temptation. He did, indeed, cry out for the set down Ashtead so longed to see him receive. But not far from them stood one of the gentlemen who had wagered on her abilities only the previous night.

She forced a laugh that she hoped sounded natural. "It seems all I have done since my arrival in Brighton is to play piquet. Forgive me, but not tonight."

Out of the corner of her eye, she saw the buck lose interest and wander away. So did George Yarborough, leaving her with Ashtead. A puzzled frown creased his brow, and she scanned the room, seeking inspiration for some topic with which to divert him. She saw Mrs. Hester Winslow in conversation with her Uncle Marmaduke, and there was Sir William Jacoby, looking quite elegant in an evening costume that would not have shamed Ashtead.

Jacoby? Presentable? She voiced the question that filled her mind. "Whatever has happened to Sir William?"

The corner of Ashtead's mouth quirked into a wry smile. "He hired a new valet yesterday, and has told the fellow to be firm with him."

Yesterday? Had he heard Lydia's murmured comment?

Even if he had, it amazed Eddie that he had acted upon it, and so swiftly. "Is Lydia here?" she asked abruptly.

"She chose to stay home this night. Too much racketing about, she said." He cast an enigmatic glance at her. "Perhaps you suffer from the same complaint? Or do you think a glass of champagne might put the fighting spirit back into you?" He took her by the elbow and propelled her away from the crowd in which they stood.

He'd get her alone soon, she realized, if not tonight, then tomorrow. And then he'd demand an explanation of her refusal to play with Yarborough. If he discovered the truth— Her stomach clenched. He would insist upon her abandoning her gaming altogether. She could not bear that, not when she drew so close to her victory, her freedom. She concentrated very hard upon thinking up some reasonable tale he might believe, but was still floundering when her Uncle Marmaduke joined them.

That gentleman cast a conspiratorial glance about, as if assuring that the three of them stood apart with no one to overhear. "Champing at the bit to get back to piquet?" he demanded with his usual joviality if unusually hushed tone.

Ashtead looked from one to the other of them, his eyes narrowing. "She just turned down a perfect opportunity."

Marmaduke shook his head sadly. "Wretched luck. But never you mind, m'girl. Just give it another day or two, then don't play every night. You'll be right as rain." Nodding to them both, he meandered off.

Ashtead's gaze rested on the flamboyant figure as Marmaduke returned to his Aunt Hester's side. Eddie considered slipping away, but knew it would do her no good. Dear Uncle Marmaduke. He'd really sunk her into the mire this time.

Ashtead turned back to her, his mouth curved in a smile that did nothing to soften the glint of steel in his eyes. "The explanation is bound to be fascinating."

To show fear or dismay would be deadly. Instead, and with a considerable effort, she waved the matter aside with an airy hand. "It is nothing of any great import. Uncle Marmaduke thought he overheard two gentlemen placing a wager on whether or not I should win, so I decided not to play for a few nights. And it has worked already," she added, seeing the flash of anger in his eyes. She told him of the buck who had lost interest in her.

Ashtead's jaw clenched in a grim line. "I'll not have your name bandied about."

She bit back the impulse to tell him it was none of his concern; he had made her his concern, and she knew him well enough now to know just how stubborn he could be. Instead, she raised her eyebrows and said, with just a hint of coldness, *"I* will not have my name bandied about."

A long moment passed. Then; "It seems you have the matter well in hand. You will do me one favor, if you will, though."

She regarded him with suspicion. "And what might that be?"

"Defeat George Yarborough soundly at your first opportunity." He nodded to her and strode off.

She stared after him, amazed. Did this mean he would refrain from meddling? Allow her to handle her own concerns in her own manner? Show respect for her wishes and abilities? Or did he mean to meddle behind her back, without her knowledge? She wished she knew.

She still hadn't decided two nights later when she at last took her seat opposite George Yarborough and watched him deal the cards. Ashtead took a seat at a table nearby, playing with her Uncle Marmaduke. The later gave her a sly wink, then turned his attention to trying to separate the viscount from what few funds he possessed.

Eddie concentrated on Yarborough, rising at last from the table with almost four hundred pounds stuffed into her reticule. She thanked him, hoped Ashtead noted well the man's dazed look, and turned away. Immediately another young buck presented himself; one of those who had wagered on her abilities. She thanked him but declined, saying she wearied of the pastime, and headed back into the withdrawing room, where a young lady performed upon a harp, accompanied by another on the German flute.

Eddie paused, lost in the beauty of the sound, her eyes closing as she gave herself over to a magic almost as potent as Xanthe's humming. The last notes lingered in the air, fading slowly, only to be interrupted by the polite applause of the audience. Then everyone seemed to be moving, leaving their chairs, crossing the room, reforming their small knots of conversation. An interval in the evening's entertainment, it seemed.

Ashtead walked past her, not even slowing as he murmured, "Thank you."

Eddie smiled to herself as she crossed the room to where Lydia sat beside her Aunt Hester. Her friend seemed unusually distracted, Eddie noted. She took the seat beside her and tried a tactic normally guaranteed to interest the other lady. "Was that not the loveliest duet?"

"Indeed, it was." Lydia leaned toward her, lowering her voice. "Have you seen Sir William? I vow, I was never more surprised. He appears quite elegant."

Eddie followed the direction of Lydia's gesture, to where Jacoby sat alone, not far away, gazing thoughtfully into space. Eddie had not seen his black coat before—unless it was one that had been cleaned and pressed beyond recognition. The hand of a master had tied his neckcloth, and a glint of a ruby showed in its snowy folds. He would never be handsome, of course, but he could be quite striking. "Now, if only he could be induced to notice his fellow guests, or even the entertainment," Eddie whispered back.

"He is writing!" protested Lydia. "I own, I had not expected him to come out when he is at such a difficult stage of his work. For him to have done so, and to have taken such pains with his appearance, is the greatest compliment to our hostess."

It was not their hostess, but Lydia who deserved this compliment, Eddie suspected.

As the evening progressed, her suspicions increased that Lydia's concern for Jacoby was not entirely of a maternal nature. Fascinated, she watched as that gentleman emerged from his reverie, noted Lydia's presence, and made his way at once to her side. Lydia looked up at him with a smile that managed to combine warmth with a touch of shyness. Now, if Jacoby would just engage her in a lively conversation, perhaps bring her a glass of punch— Jacoby seated himself, nodded absently at the comment Lydia addressed to him, and slipped back into his literary reverie. Lydia sighed, and fetched refreshments for herself and her Aunt Hester.

Concern for her friend's affairs soon gave way to concern for her own. For the next two nights, Eddie steadfastly refused all invitations to piquet. She chafed at the delay; with every passing day, her time raced away. And now that she must show discretion, she won less money, and won less often.

On the third night, she permitted herself to attend a card party, aware every moment that she would have to show extreme caution. A solemn-faced butler admitted them to the house, and a babble of voices drifted down from the floor above, announcing the presence of a large number of people. Her presence would be unremarkable among so many other guests. Relieved, she ascended to the drawing room, where the reassuring sight of her Uncle Marmaduke greeted her. He waved, then returned his attention to his cards. And there, on the opposite side of the room, sat Captain Kennilworth with George Elliston.

So the man who rarely lost was here tonight. Perhaps she could make his acquaintance at last. Mr. Elliston would introduce her, and if Uncle Marmaduke or Ashtead did not intervene, she might be able to pit her skill against his. And she wanted to do that, very much indeed. Considering the stakes he seemed to prefer, she might be able to win sufficient sums to make up for the nights she had dared not play.

Jacoby sat nearby, for once aware of his company, just finishing a game of piquet with Colonel Chesterfield. He looked up, murmured an excuse to Chesterfield, and strode over to her side. After the usual polite greetings, he asked, as casually as he could manage, "Are your cousins to be present this night?"

"Are they not here yet?" That meant Ashtead could not prevent her from playing with Kennilworth, if she sought him out quickly.

George Elliston, with whom she had not played for almost two weeks, interrupted them, gaily demanding a chance to take his revenge. That meant Kennilworth was also free. Perhaps, after one game, she might induce Elliston to present her to his former partner.

They played out their hands quickly, with Eddie the winner by a great many points. Elliston's cheerful complaints at what he called her infernal luck attracted the attention of players at the neighboring tables, and even though his apparently endless wealth and inability to win at piquet made him an excellent opponent for her, she declined another game. She stood, only to find herself facing the darkly handsome Captain Kennilworth himself.

He looked her over with an appreciative smile lighting his flashing brown eyes, then turned to her erstwhile partner. "You must present me." Elliston did, and Captain Kennilworth took Eddie's hand, carrying it to his lips. "I am charmed to meet the lady whom I hear rarely loses at piquet."

So she had a reputation that matched his. It didn't please her, but at least it had brought him to her, requesting the game she so greatly desired. She looked him over appraisingly, suddenly nervous.

George Elliston rose. "Take my place." He clasped Eddie's hand. "Kennilworth is too full of himself," he told her cheerfully. "He can stand being taken down a peg." He slapped the captain on the shoulder, and moved away.

Captain Kennilworth gestured toward the chair she had just vacated. Something in his manner, in the steadfast way he studied her, assessing her, left her uneasy. She couldn't rid herself of the growing conviction she made a grave error in playing with him.

By the end of the first hand, she found herself ahead by barely twenty points. She watched him covertly as he gathered the cards once more. His manners were charming, his address certain to please, yet the strange sensation of disquiet that had settled over her continued to grow. It would be best, she decided, if she played no more than the single game with him.

Several of the other guests gathered about them, watching, laughing, calling encouragement to her or to the captain. He acknowledged the comments with a smile that grew increasingly tighter as Eddie took trick after trick. He did not like to lose, that was obvious, particularly before so many witnesses. For a moment Eddie considered misplaying intentionally, but the stakes had grown with each hand, and she dared not cast her hard-won money to the winds.

As their sixth hand finally played out, she wanted only to escape. She would willingly mis-tally her points, try to claim a near draw, anything to stem his swelling anger. It frightened her, for she sensed a ruthlessness in him against which she felt powerless. But several of the gentlemen who stood around their table had kept a running score as well, and now shouted with delight as they pronounced Eddie's staggering total.

Kennilworth's knuckles whitened as his hands clenched the edge of the table. "It seems your reputation falls short of the truth, Lady Edwina. You *never* lose."

"That is nonsense." She tried to force a lightness into her voice. "You permitted me to win, which was most chivalrous of you."

For a moment, she thought he would allow her words to stand, allow himself to save face before so many witnesses. He seemed to hover on the brink of doing so; then his complexion darkened. He rose, tall and menacing, and Eddie shrank back in her seat.

He smiled; had he been an animal, he would have displayed fangs. "My congratulations. This time, you

have won. But I promise you, I will have my revenge."
With that, he tossed her a purse without bothering to
count the contents and pushed his way through the
crowd.

Eddie closed her eyes, feeling physically ill.

Eight

Ashtead strolled along the Steyne, only vaguely aware of the other members of the *ton* who took part in the early morning promenade. His thoughts traveled far from the warm sunshine that bathed the scene; they centered on Edwina, on her laughter, her grace, her single-minded determination. It seemed likely, even with all the obstacles she must face, that she would win her competence. Then when she had, would she stubbornly cling to her hard-won independence, or would she be willing to compromise it for love?

He had noted the way her gaze strayed to him when she thought he was not aware. It had occurred to him she might not be as indifferent to him as she would like him to believe. But as long as he remained in need of a fortune, she would never allow herself to trust him. Which meant that somehow, short of marrying an heiress, he must discover a means of running his grandfather's vast holdings without recourse to his vast income.

A pity he lacked Edwina's talent with the cards. Copying her endeavors would net him a tidy sum in very short order, for he would have no need to exercise the cautions she must employ to protect her name. But though he knew himself to be a good player, he was not her equal.

His thoughts returned to the estates, to the many obligations and holdings of the Marquis of Shoreham. His great-uncle's agent, Bentley, knew every detail of their management. Perhaps he might have some suggestions on how to make them self-supporting that his great-uncle had so far rejected. On impulse, Ashtead headed into the Castle Inn, which stood on the opposite side of the street, to write the agent a letter upon the instant.

He entered the lobby, only to encounter Bentley in person, standing to one side of the room with the clerk who managed the hotel. Now, here was a fortuitous turn of events. Then his satisfaction faded. Bentley, a thin man of advancing middle years, whose sole purpose in life seemed to be service to the irascible Marquis of Shoreham, would never have journeyed to Brighton on any pleasure expedition. He had come for a purpose, and that purpose could only have to do with his master.

Memory of the old gentleman on what he'd claimed to be his deathbed flooded back. Ashtead hadn't believed him that frail, but it was possible his granddaughter's defiance had brought on an apoplectic fit. He strode forward, seriously alarmed, calling the man's name.

Bentley turned from the clerk and stared at Ashtead. The deep lines about his brow and eyes eased. "My lord." He hurried forward with a flattering eagerness. "I did not think to find you here."

"How does the old gentleman?" Ashtead demanded.

The thin face primmed. "As well as can be expected. He has not been pleased with recent events."

The worst of his fears alleviated, Ashtead smiled. "Rare fit of temper?"

Bentley pursed his mouth. "We took the precaution of summoning his doctor."

"I'll wager he cursed you soundly for your efforts."

"Yes, m'lord. And the doctor as well." They fell silent a moment, contemplating his lordship's less than cordial relationship with his physician. "Mr. Salton recommended cupping," Bentley added.

"No, did he?" Ashtead grinned. "How very brave of him. And did my great-uncle submit to it?"

"No, my lord, I am sorry to say he did not. He also expressed his disinterest in undergoing the procedure at any time in the future as well."

"So I may presume it is not cupping that has brought you to Brighton."

"No." Bentley cleared his throat. "It is Lady Edwina."

Poor Edwina. Ashtead glanced around, but the room seemed far too full of people for any conversation of a delicate nature. He drew his great-uncle's man of affairs from the lobby and into one of the more private salons. "How angry with her is he?"

Bentley appeared acutely uncomfortable. "He is not pleased, my lord."

"Of course he isn't. I doubt she has ever defied him before in her entire life. For that matter, I am very probably the only person who ever has."

Bentley cleared his throat. "I fear he is much accustomed to having everything ordered precisely as he should wish. Which makes it somewhat—awkward, shall we say?—when someone opposes him."

"Especially when that someone has always bowed to his every whim." He studied the gloss on his Hessians, only partially aware of the lights and colors reflected in their gleaming surface. 'What are your orders?"

"To bring her back with me, my lord. And in truth, I hope she will come."

Ashtead's gaze narrowed on him. "Why?"

Bentley's discomfort increased. "He does not tolerate defiance." The man peered up at him, his expression intent. "Do you remember Lady Almeria?"

Ashtead frowned, racking a memory that brought forth no connection.

Bentley nodded, somber. "His own daughter, and he has not allowed her name to be mentioned in the Castle for nigh on twenty-five years."

Fascinated, Ashtead asked, "What did she do?"

"Rejected the marriage he had arranged for her. It seems she had fallen in love with a soldier. An admirable young gentleman in every respect, the heir to a barony, with lands and rents of his own. But he was not your great-uncle's choice, and so he threatened to cut Lady Almeria out of his will."

"I take it she eloped with her soldier."

Bentley nodded. "She hoped he would come to accept her marriage, especially when her husband won renown in the wars, but he would not hear either of their names. It was as if she had never been born. And so lovely and full of life as she was."

"He doted on her?" Ashtead hazarded.

Bentley blinked. "No. I could not say that he cared particularly for either of his children. He simply demanded their complete obedience. Which is why"—and he wrung his hands together—"it is so very important for Lady Edwina to return at once."

"He will make her life even more miserable than it was before," Ashtead pointed out.

"But if she does come immediately, and begs his pardon humbly, perhaps even admits she was wrong to defy him, he might deign to be forgiving and not disinherit her. And she has no other source of income. If she will not come at his bidding, he will deny her any support, any dowry. I very much fear for her future."

"And if she does return, will he still expect her to wed me? Or does he hold me to blame for her running away?"

Bentley avoided his gaze. "He does not believe you did anything amiss, my lord."

A snort of derisive laughter escaped Ashtead. "Good God, does he not? You have more sense than that, I'll wager."

Bentley cleared his throat. "It is not for me to say, my lord."

"It seems none of us are to have any say except my great-uncle." He considered a moment. "Has it occurred to him that I might refuse to wed Lady Edwina?"

"He—he expressed himself in such terms as made that seem highly possible, my lord."

"He did, did he?" Ashtead smiled, then his amusement faded. "Do you know what he plans?"

"It seems possible, my lord—possible, I say, not definite—that his lordship might decide to leave the majority, if not all, of his fortune to you."

"I see." His great-uncle would cut out Edwina because of her defiance, while he, who had caused the poor girl to erupt in this sole aberration against her grandfather, would reap the benefit. He could have the monies he desperately needed for the estate. But what if the old gentleman still demanded the marriage between them? That was highly probable. He was not one to allow himself to be beaten. The monies could still be lost to them both.

Of course, if the marquis knew of Edwina's attempts to win her independence from him at the gaming tables, he would cast her off utterly, as if she had never existed.

That would leave the fortune to him, without any ties or conditions.

His jaw tightened. He would not betray her; he had to make certain the marquis never learned of what Edwina was doing. There were, as he well knew, funds enough to share between them. She could be more than comfortable on a small fraction of the inheritance. She could command the elegancies of life, buy costly gowns, attend an endless round of parties. She need not exist in that tiny cottage on whatever pittance of an interest her winnings would produce. All she had to do was return home.

And possibly face another arranged marriage. He knew his great-uncle all too well. The old gentleman would not be satisfied until he had forced the girl to bend to his will, to admit herself wrong in defying him, to accept—with an appropriate show of meekness—whatever new decisions he made about her life.

No, Ashtead would not allow that. Somehow, he would make certain Edwina had her chance to choose her own future.

"It will be best," he said slowly as an idea came to him, "for you to see her, I suppose."

"Indeed it will." Bentley regarded him hopefully.

"Then you will be able to assure her grandfather that she is in eminently respectable hands. They are probably at home this morning."

They arrived at the house on the Marine Parade to find the two ladies on the verge of departure. Xanthe was humming one of those delightful tunes he had never been able to place. She stepped forward, and the melody seemed to linger in the air as she welcomed Mr. Bentley and led the way into the salon. The estate agent followed, a smile on his face for the first time since Ashtead had encountered him that day. The warmth of Lady Xanthe's charm often seemed to have that effect on people.

Ashtead took up a position behind Edwina's chair, and leaned forward to murmur in her ear. "This could not have been better. He will give a glowing report to your grandfather."

Edwina cast him a dubious glance over her shoulder. "How long does Mr. Bentley intend to remain in Brighton?"

"He will probably return to the Castle in the morning," he reassured her.

"If any mention of my gaming should chance to reach his ears—" She broke off, eyeing Ashtead in no little concern.

His hand rested on her shoulder for a moment. "I shall see to it he meets no one who might betray you."

She stared at him, her expression one of hope mingling with lingering uncertainty. It tugged at his heart. Poor child, did she have so little faith in anyone's willingness to help her? Certainly no one had ever defied her grandfather successfully before. The determination grew in him that she would have her independence.

Yet he could not, he realized in frustration, simply promise her a share of the fortune if he should inherit it. That would make her feel under an obligation to him, a situation that neither of them could tolerate. No, if she were to become independent, she must do it on her own. And then— Well, he would see.

When Ashtead and Bentley at last took their leave, Bentley walked in silence for some time. "Lady Xanthe is a delightful woman," he said at last. "I cannot remember ever having the pleasure of making her acquaintance before, and can only regret there is no hostess at the Castle to make it possible for her to come to stay with Lady Edwina. If only the girl had asked to pay this visit instead of running away, but then—" He broke off, the sudden flush to his cheeks indicating he might have recollected the reason for Edwina's precipitous departure.

"You may also tell her grandfather," said Ashtead, playing his last card, "that Lady Edwina and I are in constant company with one another. If he would but allow her to remain for a few weeks longer, I might be able to gratify his original desires and announce our engagement before the end of summer."

"You are trying to fix your interest with her?" demanded Bentley, for once forgetting the deference due his future employer.

"It is my very great desire to make Lady Edwina my wife," he declared, with far more truth than he could have ever believed possible.

Eddie tied the ribands of her chip-straw bonnet at an angle that indicated a jauntiness she was far from feeling. Two days had passed since Mr. Bentley had returned to the Castle. He had called upon them before taking his departure, renewing his assurances that he would do everything in his power to reconcile her grandfather to her continued absence. Eddie had her doubts that anyone could convince her grandfather to see reason, but she kept her mouth closed. Xanthe had promised her eight weeks, and she didn't doubt the fairy's ability to keep even so redoubtable an opponent as the Marquis of Shoreham at bay until the terms of their agreement had been met.

But she didn't want her grandfather unduly distressed either. She would never be able to forgive herself if her actions drove him into an apoplectic fit. That it would be his own fault for a lifetime of autocratic decrees and considering no one's interests but his own made the matter no better.

When she descended the stairs, she did not see Xanthe, who had announced her intention to do absolutely nothing that afternoon. Assuming this meant the fairy would be entertaining herself in some magical and frivolous manner, Eddie set forth alone for the short walk to the house rented by Mrs. Hester Winslow. There, Edgarth opened the door, and showed her into the salon, where Lydia stood at the window, her usually erect posture drooped in dejection.

Lydia turned as the butler announced Eddie, and forced a weak smile to her lips, then abandoned the effort. "Oh, it is of all things the most deplorable," she announced.

Eddie, in a probably misguided attempt at humor, cast a rapid glance over her appearance. "I thought this gown looked quite fetching on me."

Lydia shook her head. "You are as bad as Ashtead!"

"Pray, do not resort to insults." Eddie came forward. "Tell me what has occurred."

"Oh, it is of no great moment. It is just so very typical of him." Lydia slumped into a chair.

"Ashtead?" Eddie inquired, all sympathy.

"No, goose. Jacoby. He promised quite faithfully he should drive out into the countryside with Aunt Hester and me, but he did not come at the appointed time, and when I sent Ashtead to his hotel, he was not there. Gentlemen can be so very vexatious!"

"Perhaps he mistook the day."

"It would be wonderful if he did not." Lydia glared at her clasped hands. "I can only wonder why we poor females ever subject ourselves to the society of men. I vow, I want no more of them."

"Perhaps you should have sent him a note this morning to remind him," Eddie suggested.

Lydia's mouth thinned. "If a gentleman thinks so little of"—she broke off, her cheeks flushing—"of his engagements," she went on hurriedly, "I can see no reason to remind him. He would prove the most dreadful companion. Indeed I cannot think why we even bothered to invite him, except that Aunt Hester thought he might find it pleasant."

The door's opening at that moment spared Eddie the necessity of answering. She turned to see who entered just as Edgarth announced Jacoby himself. That gentleman strolled into the room, an amiable smile on his face.

"Lady Harcourt." He sketched her a bow. "And Lady Edwina." This called for another bow. "Good morning."

"It is afternoon," Lydia responded coldly.

"Is it?" He sounded surprised. "Well, at least I have turned myself out in prime rig."

"Indeed you have." Eddie could only admire the determination of a valet who could have wrought such a change in the man's appearance.

"*Why* have you?" Lydia's voice showed no trace of thawing.

Jacoby frowned. "Can't remember. Good thing that I did, though. Encountered Miss Marlowe, and she said I looked all the crack."

"Indeed." Lydia's eyes kindled, but she let the mention of Miss Marlowe pass. "Do you perhaps recall some scheme about driving out into the countryside?"

He blinked at her. "However did you know about that? I spent most of the morning working out a scene on that idea for the final act. Dashed if it won't make all the difference to the play."

Eddie closed her eyes, waiting for Lydia's storm to break over the poor man's head.

Pregnant silence reigned for a full half minute. Then, in a voice of marveling wonder, she said, "What a truly original idea. Have you ever considered taking such a drive yourself?"

"A—" He broke off, considering. "Why not? Would you care to go tomorrow, Lady Harcourt?"

With an exclamation of vexation, Lydia shot up from her chair and marched out of the room, leaving Jacoby staring after her in puzzlement. When the door slammed behind her, he looked to Eddie. "Did I say something amiss?"

Eddie regarded him with a measure of her friend's exasperation. "You had pledged yourself to drive out with her and Mrs. Winslow this morning."

His brow lowered. "Had I? Lord, no wonder she is angry. What a mull I have made of it. Would she permit me to apologize, do you think?"

"You may certainly try."

"It's this damn—dashed play, you see." A note of eagerness crept into his voice. "You see, in the last act—"

Eddie held up her hand. "You should address your apology to Lady Harcourt."

"Yes, of course." Jacoby fell silent. "But it is the play, you see," he went on after a moment. "When I write, I can think of nothing else, and what occurs in my own life becomes inextricably confused with what goes on in the play. But I'll have finished it soon—within a week or two, I should think. And when I am not writing, I behave in a perfectly normal manner, and have no difficulty keeping track of my appointments, or especially the people, only then. . . ." His voice trailed off and the faraway look crept back into his eyes.

"Only then a new idea strikes you?" Eddie suggested.

"What?" He blinked and refocused on her.

"Never mind," Eddie told him.

"There is an important person," he informed her with considerable force, and on that cryptic utterance took his leave.

And so he had returned to his labors. Except he had never been far from them. Poor Lydia. She had passed quickly from looking upon Jacoby's vagaries with a tolerant eye. Now they seemed to distress her. Love had a disconcerting tendency to creep up on one and utterly destroy one's peace. Why must gentlemen prove so exasperating?

Eddie still contemplated Jacoby's haphazard behavior and Ashtead's continuing attentions to herself the following afternoon as she stood before the shelves in Donaldson's Lending Library. None of the titles appealed to her; what she needed, she supposed, was a guidebook, rather like the ones available to visitors to London or Bath. Except what she wanted was one that explained the male sex. She sighed and turned away, her thoughts once more returning to the probably mercenary motive behind Ashtead's flattering gallantries.

The unusually rapid approach of booted footsteps within this sanctuary dragged her from her reverie, and she looked up to see Ashtead's tall, elegant figure striding toward her. Her heart lifted, only to sink once more into a morass of confusion. He didn't look pleased. In fact, he looked furious about something. Frantically, she searched her memory for any actions or words on her part that might have brought on this mood, but found none. With growing trepidation, she waited.

"There you are." He took her arm in a tight grip and drew her into a quiet corner. "Bentley is back."

Relief that his anger was not directed at her vied with the sudden fear brought on by the urgency of his manner. She could think of no reason why Mr. Bentley's return should perturb him, unless— "My—my grandfather. Is he—"

"Furious." Ashtead's mouth tightened. "Every new setback seems to grant him greater vigor."

She let out the breath she hadn't realized she was holding. "I—I feared—"

The glint in his eyes softened. "I am sorry to have given you a bad moment. No, he seems to be quite well and as malevolent as ever."

She digested this. "Then why has Mr. Bentley returned?"

"It seems that one of your grandfather's friends—I am not privileged to know whom—has taken it upon himself to inform your grandfather that you spend every evening at the gaming tables, playing for ruinously high stakes."

She blanched. "I—I don't." But she knew her protest to be pointless. Her grandfather believed it, and that was enough. The forthcoming interview with Mr. Bentley would not be pleasant, but she would have to face it. She straightened her shoulders. "Where is he?"

"When I saw him, he was headed toward your house."

She nodded. "We had best return at once."

"Good girl. It is always best to meet the enemy head-on."

"Is it? I merely find I would rather know the worst

at once. Dreading it can be even more distressing than knowing for certain."

Yet when it came right down to it, what difference would this interview make? Her grandfather could not force her to return to the Castle. Xanthe would see to that. But she did not want to be at daggers drawn with her closest relative, the old man whom she had tended and depended upon for so very long. The old man, she reminded herself grimly, who had treated her with so little concern that he could have demanded her marriage to a gentleman she could neither like nor esteem.

That gentleman, she remembered with an odd tug, had been Ashtead.

And she had come to both like and esteem him very much indeed.

In fact, had her sensibilities not been repulsed by the offer's being made solely because of the fortune, had he not been as outraged as she to the point where he had drunk himself into near oblivion to be able to swallow his pride and accept the outrageous demand— In short, had she been allowed to come to know Ashtead first, had he paid her court, the situation might have been very different.

They found Xanthe and made their rapid way back to the house on the Marine Parade, where Mr. Bentley paced the salon floor, Titus his only companion. The immense feline sprawled before an open window, sunning himself. He blinked sleepy eyes at Xanthe, and just the tip of his tail twitched. A smile tugged at the fairy's mouth, which she suppressed with difficulty. What, Eddie wondered, had Titus just told her?

Mr. Bentley strode forward and bowed over Xanthe's hand, his expression a mixture of acute discomfort and embarrassment. His gaze fell on Ashtead, and a mute plea lit his eyes, an appeal from one male to another.

Ashtead merely leaned against the wall, folding his arms, waiting.

"What may we do for you?" Xanthe glided to her favorite chair, and waved Mr. Bentley to the one opposite. An empty wineglass stood beside it, mute testimony to the strain of his waiting.

Eddie crossed to the decanter and poured another glass. It was tempting to drink it herself, for she didn't want to face the inevitable unpleasantness. Resolutely, she carried it to Ashtead, then returned to refill Mr. Bentley's. She met Xanthe's humorous, rueful gaze, then gave in to temptation and splashed out a small amount for herself.

Mr. Bentley didn't appear to notice this eccentricity. He looked down at his shoes, not meeting her gaze. "I have come from the marquis," he announced quite unnecessarily.

Xanthe gave him an encouraging smile. "I trust his lordship is enjoying tolerable health?"

One of Titus's ears flicked.

Mr. Bentley grasped at this offering. "We fear greatly for him."

"If he controlled his temper, you need not," Ashtead pointed out.

Mr. Bentley threw him a pleading look. "He—he is much vexed over news that has reached him. He fears Lady Edwina may have fallen in with company not suited to her rank and gentle upbringing. He has heard that her uncle . . ."

Eddie bristled. "My uncle—" she began, but met Ashtead's warning glance and subsided.

Mr. Bentley cleared his throat. "Your grandfather regards this as a very grave matter, my dear Lady Edwina. He has sent me to escort you home."

"Then he has sent you on a fruitless errand." It wasn't easy to get the words out. Disobeying while in the heat of passion was one thing. To defy her autocratic grandfather with calm deliberation was quite another.

Mr. Bentley turned to the fairy. "Lady Xanthe, you are a gentlewoman of excellent good sense. You must see the seriousness of allowing her to be at such odds with her grandfather, her natural guardian. I ask that you reason with her."

"And if not, for her to throw me out so I will have no choice but to go back?" Eddie demanded.

A deep flush crept upward from Mr. Bentley's collar. "If you remain adamant, my poor child, it is to be hoped that your godmother, at least, can see the need for your compliance."

"Actually, I do not," said Xanthe with a calm that seemed to leave Mr. Bentley speechless.

He stared at her, his mouth open, for several seconds. "But—but surely—" He broke off, unable to give voice to his disbelief.

Titus leapt onto Xanthe's lap and settled himself to his satisfaction. The fairy's hands stroked the long fur. "The choice," she said softly, "is entirely up to Edwina."

Mr. Bentley turned to her. "Please, Lady Edwina. Your grandfather's health—"

"It seems that temper does him good." Edwina hesitated, feeling the old compunction to submit, to do as she was ordered. Only not this time. She shook her head. "There are still two more weeks of my visit to Brighton. I shall not return until that time is complete." And not even then, she hoped, but she refrained from voicing that thought.

"You cannot have considered the consequences—" he began.

She held up her hand. "Indeed I have. I do not believe he will carry himself off in an apoplectic fit. And as for other considerations . . . They do not weigh with me. I will not return at this time, and there is nothing you can say that will make me change my mind."

Mr. Bentley looked helplessly toward Xanthe, who merely smiled. His gaze traveled on to Ashtead.

The viscount shook his head. "Don't look at me. My complying with his orders is what brought this about in the first place. I have no intention of meddling again."

"But you know what he will do," Mr. Bentley protested.

Ashtead turned to Eddie. "He means that your grandfather may well disinherit you."

She shrugged. "So much the better for you then."

Bentley remained for nearly half an hour more, trying whatever persuasions came to his mind, but Eddie remained firm. At last Ashtead saw him out, and Eddie slipped away to her room, drained.

She had burned her last bridge. If she failed to win her independence, she would have nowhere else to turn. But she couldn't have simply given up, not when she was this close to her success. But if ultimately she failed—

No, she couldn't face that thought. If she did not succeed at her gaming scheme, she had no idea what she would do. Xanthe had granted her an opportunity, not a solution. Which, she knew, meant she must make the most of her one and only chance to win her independence. This night, she determined, she would resume her gaming with a discreet vengeance.

Nine

On the second floor of the Castle, Ashtead strode through the antechamber with its medicine bottles and daybed, then entered the darkened apartment beyond. Stebbings had drawn the draperies against the early afternoon sun, but a branch of candles stood on the bedside table. Their wavering light threw into sharp relief the frail figure propped on pillows in the massive canopied bed. One of the fragile hands held a reading glass, the other a well-thumbed volume. Ashtead doubted it would be anything of an improving or uplifting nature, but could not resist raising his eyebrows. "What, have you resorted to reading sermons? The end must be nearer than I thought."

The Marquis of Shoreham lowered the book to the bedcovers and cast a malevolent look at his visitor. "Hah!" His gaze narrowed on him. "So, you've come back, have you? Brought my granddaughter?"

Ashtead drew an elaborately decorated enameled snuff box from his pocket and flicked it open with his thumb. "Care to try my sort?" He held it out.

Shoreham took it in one gnarled, arthritic hand and sniffed. He frowned, sniffed again, helped himself to a pinch, then sneezed with vigor. With irritated, flapping fingers, he brushed away the fragments that had fallen to his lap. "Passable," came his grudging verdict. "Where is she? Why didn't she come to me at once?" A touch of eagerness shone in his rheumy eyes.

"Do you miss her?" Ashtead helped himself to a pinch, then returned the box to his pocket.

"Damned, foolish question." Shoreham glared at him. "Where is she?"

"Tending—quite properly—to several engagements from which she could not cry off."

Shoreham's narrowed gaze focused on him, remaining there for an uncomfortably long time. "She didn't come," he said at last.

For a fleeting moment Ashtead read disappointment there. This emotion faded at once, to be replaced by cold anger. "What the devil does she mean, defying her own grandfather? She'll come home *now.*"

"Not unless you want to cause a great deal of gossip," Ashtead countered. He was by no means certain of the success of this ploy, but he had come with one purpose in mind, and he intended to fulfill it.

"Hah!" repeated the marquis. Then; "If you didn't escort her, what the devil do you mean by coming here yourself?"

"To convey her apologies for—"

"Apologies?" Shoreham snorted. "For trying to drive her poor old grandfather into the grave?"

"For not being able to pay you the visit you requested at this time," Ashtead finished smoothly.

"Visit?" The old man's face darkened. "I told her to come home. At once. Or did that fool Bentley soften my words? If he did, I'll make him wish he were never born."

"He didn't." Lord, this was getting difficult, trying to

protect both Bentley and Edwina. "But my cousin has, as I have said, a number of engagements that—"

" Damn her engagements! I told her to come home, and she has defied me!" He glowered at the hands that clenched and unclenched in his lap. Abruptly, he muttered, "Leave me!" and collapsed back against the pillows.

Ashtead turned on his heel and strode from the room. In the antechamber he told the hovering Stebbings to take a cordial into his master. Then he let himself into the hall. No serious concerns for his great-uncle haunted him; his collapse had borne the stamp of an enfeebled autocrat playing off one of the few tricks that remained to him.

A brisk ride around the countryside, on a mount borrowed from the stables, did much to ease Ashtead's troubled mood. It had dawned on him some hours previously that Edwina was not likely to appreciate all the trouble he took on her behalf. She might even actively resent it. Well, he would face that hurdle when he reached it. Right now he must try again to intervene for her.

He dined in solitary state; Mr. Bentley, who might normally have joined him, had absented himself. Ashtead was sorry. He would very much have liked to spend some time discussing alternative means of financing the vast Shoreham holdings and commitments. As it was, all he did was contemplate the interview Lo come, and try to limit the amount of wine and brandy he imbibed. It occurred to him that 'such an evening, as, this normally would have revolted him. But he didn't begrudge the boredom, not if it served to help Edwina.

He returned to his great-uncle's chamber as soon as he finished the meal. The marquis did not appear to have moved since he last saw him; he still lay against the pillows, but now his gleaming, malevolent eyes fixed on the door. "You didn't waste any time," he said, as the valet ushered Ashtead within.

"I've been warned not to keep you sitting up late." He seated himself in the chair that Stebbings had drawn up at the bedside.

"Hah!" Shoreham glared at him. "Bunch of old women. I'll do a long time yet."

"To be sure you will, if only to annoy the lot of them," Ashtead agreed with marked cordiality.

"Hah!" repeated the marquis, though this time he sounded pleased. "Where are the cards?" The elderly man's scowl returned. "What the devil is my girl about, gaming as if she were some curst Captain Sharp?"

Ashtead found the desired deck on the bedside table and shuffled. "Enjoying the activity *you* taught her to love." Ashtead kept his voice light. "Only the worst of the gossipmongers would try to make more of it than that. Her skill does you credit, and your enemies find fault with it."

The old man's gaze rested on him. "Are you trying to tell me she's not gaming every night?"

Ashtead looked up from his dealing, raising his eyebrows. "Who tried to tell you that? She plays perhaps three or four evenings a week, usually no more than a game or two unless she's attending a card party."

Shoreham glared at his cards, made his discards, and declared his points. They played out their hand, and the marquis took the last trick with a snort. "Well, she plays a damn sight better than you do."

"So I have discovered."

The marquis shot him a penetrating glance. "So it's true? You're keeping an eye on her?"

"You may be sure of it." He gathered the cards and shuffled again.

The marquis watched Ashtead's rapidly moving fingers. "Bentley told me you were still trying to marry the chit."

"I would be honored," Ashtead said, and the intensity behind his words surprised him, "if she would consent to be my wife."

"Hah!" The marquis ignored the cards Ashtead dealt. "Piqued your pride, did she? Probably not many who'd reject you, even drunk as a wheelbarrow. Or is it the money?"

Ashtead's teeth clenched. "It is not."

Shoreham snorted, and his lip curled into a smile. "Be damned to her. The money's yours. No need to marry that baggage of a granddaughter of mine. Make your life a misery, as like as not."

Ashtead looked up from the hand he organized. "Like as not, my life will be a misery without her."

Shoreham stared at him, then for the first time in Ashtead's memory, burst out laughing.

Ashtead returned to Brighton the following morning in no good mood. He had spent an unreasonable portion of the night arguing with his great-uncle, but the old gentleman had refused to budge. The fortune would be left unconditionally to Ashtead, and Edwina would be cut off without a penny. "You came when I summoned her. She didn't," had become the old man's litany, until Ashtead had given up at last in disgust.

The marquis might still be induced to change his mind. If not, Ashtead would settle a sum on Edwina as soon as he inherited. That she would refuse the money, in spite of her having every right to it, he knew as a certainty. Well, he would see it put into her name. Somehow, he would make certain she shared in it. She would find him every bit as stubborn as she was herself.

As he turned onto the Marine Parade, his desire to see Edwina as soon as possible overcame his reluctance to report his failure to her. Instead of proceeding to his aunt's home, he drew up his grays before Lady Xanthe's establishment. Turning his equipage over to the groom, he mounted the steps and knocked, only to be informed by the majordomo that Lady Xanthe and her charge were not at home. The extent of his disappointment surprised him, lowering his spirits even farther.

Edgarth opened his aunt's door to him. As soon as he stepped into the hall, he heard the welcome tones of Edwina's voice, raised in laughing protest. Stopping only to cast off his curly beaver and his driving gloves, he entered the salon, where he was greeted by the sight of her, delightful in a morning gown of pale blue muslin, her hair arranged in artless ringlets. He gazed at her for a long moment, reveling in the mere sight of her, all else in the room fading to insignificance for him. She looked up, a mischievous smile lighting her eyes; he found it difficult to breathe.

"You've been gone," she said softly.

What would she do if he gathered her into his arms and kissed her? he wondered. Scream, possibly. Or more likely box his ears. He would have to put it to the test one day. His gaze met and held hers, until soft color tinged her cheeks and she looked down. Definitely, he had to put it to the test.

Recalling himself, he strode forward to kiss his aunt's

cheek, bow over Lady Xanthe's hand, smile at Lydia, and nod to Mr. Marmaduke Rutland, who sat with the ladies. "Have I interrupted a party?"

"Not in the least, dear boy." Mr. Rutland rose. "Mrs. Winslow, it is time I took my leave if I am not to be late for an engagement. Morning, Ashtead." He bowed low over his hostess's hand, holding it for a long moment, then took himself off.

"We ought to be going as well." Lady Xanthe rose. "Come, Eddie, my love."

Edwina looked as if she were about to protest, then changed her mind. She took her leave of Aunt Hester and Lydia, then turned to Ashtead. For a long moment her gaze searched his face, as if seeking the answer to some question.

He took her hand, enjoying the warmth of her touch. "I will call on you later, if I may," he said softly.

"Oh, yes. Please." She hesitated, then repeated, "Yes," and allowed him to escort her from the room.

When he returned from seeing them to the door, Aunt Hester turned to him eagerly. "Were you successful? Has Shoreham forgiven dearest Eddie?"

"No." Ashtead strode to the table and poured himself some wine. "He has cut her off without so much as a shilling."

"He cannot!" exclaimed Lydia, outraged.

"He has." Ashtead tossed off half the glass. "He would not listen to any excuse or reason, and I made many of them."

"It is monstrous!" declared Aunt Hester. "That he could turn his own granddaughter into the world with neither dowry nor support is unforgivable."

"It is also just like a man, to be so thoughtless for

the needs of another." Lydia's cheeks flushed, and she hurried from the room.

Wisdom dictated he let her be. He ignored it, and followed his sister into the hall. He found her standing on the first landing, staring up the stairs with the vacant look of one who did not see what lay before her. "What is it, Lydia?" he asked gently.

"What?" She started, then gazed down on him. "Why, whatever do you mean? What is what?"

"Whatever has you so vexed."

"Me? Vexed?" A shaky laugh escaped her. "I am simply furious with my great-uncle. And who would not be? He has treated poor Eddie shamefully, and always has." With that, she swept up the steps.

So he was not to be admitted into her confidence. He continued to his own chamber, where he set about removing the dust of the road. If Lydia wouldn't tell him what was amiss, perhaps he could gain some hint from Edwina. Which, of course, necessitated paying her that promised visit at the earliest opportunity. But when he arrived once more on Lady Xanthe's doorstep, the majordomo delivered similar news: This time, Edwina and her godmother were not expected back until evening.

And that meant he would have to wait until the ball that night at the Old Ship. It would prove an uncomfortably crowded place to exchange confidences of a delicate nature. It also seemed a long time to wait before seeing her again. In fact, the sole point in its favor was that he might be able to induce her to waltz with him. Might. He had no guarantee. She might prefer to play cards. All in all, he found it an unsatisfactory situation. He wandered off in search of masculine company.

* * *

They arrived late at the ball, due to Lydia's prolonged preparations, and he hurried his party inside, impatient to see Edwina. But he didn't see her, though he spotted Lady Xanthe gazing at the punch bowl with a mischievous smile. What the devil filled her mind? he wondered, amused by the laughter that sparkled in the woman's eyes. She turned away to face the musicians, head tilted to one side, as if she considered some weighty matter.

He strolled over to join her. "Is your goddaughter not with you?"

Lady Xanthe beamed on him. "In the card room, I believe." She hummed a lively measure, and her mouth primmed with suppressed laughter. "Why do you not join her for a hand?"

"And waste her time?" Only it wouldn't be wasting her time now. She might win as much as she needed from him. Only she'd refuse to try, the stubborn chit. And why did he appreciate that trait in her?

He wended his way through the lively crowd, greeting acquaintances, until he reached the apartment set aside for the entertainment of those who did not care to caper about to the music. It was comfortably filled—Edwina would not attract any undue notice by her presence here. His gaze moved about the room, seeking out the soft brown curls he knew so well. Would they be adorned with flowers? he wondered.

They were. Tiny white and pink rosebuds peeped out from the knot at the top of her head, cascading with her curls down to her shoulders. She wore a robe of white gauze open over an underdress of pink silk. He stood for a long moment, simply gazing at her, until she looked up, straight at him, her expression one of relief. Lord, where did the chit gain the power to leave his knees weak? He moved forward, drawn to her, wanting to take her hand in his, strip that calfskin glove from her arm, kiss each of her dainty fingers. She looked away, and the separation wrenched at him. Her partner—

He stopped in his tracks, his gaze narrowing as it focused on the man seated opposite her. Captain Thomas Kennilworth. Lord, what had ever prompted her to play with the damned fellow? And judging from that look she had directed at him, she did not enjoy herself. Why didn't she just make her excuses and leave?

"There you are." Lydia slid her hand through his arm and pulled him with her. "I vow, this is the dullest ball it has ever been my misfortune to attend. There is not a single gentleman with whom I could bear to dance."

"Really?" He scanned the room, noting several of their acquaintances upon whom Lydia normally bestowed her hand quite willingly.

"Let us go home," she said. "I have the headache."

Now, what the devil was amiss with her? Were all females behaving oddly this night, or merely those with whom he was forced to deal? He halted her determined progress. "There is still something I must do before I can leave. If you will allow me to take you to Jacoby—" He spotted his friend seated alone in a corner near the door of the card room, once again wearing that vague expression that indicated he inhabited a world of his own creation.

"Why would I ever want to speak with him?" Lydia demanded.

That got Ashtead's attention. "What's toward, Lydia?"

"Nothing!" She forced a laugh. "Whatever makes you think anything so absurd? It is just that I grow weary of Brighton."

He raised his eyebrows and waited.

She hunched a shoulder. "The town is populated by a pack of bores," she snapped. "I am sinking into *ennui*. I believe I shall return to the Court." She turned on her heel and strode off. As she passed Jacoby, she picked up the fan that lay on the table at his side. The glare she directed at that gentleman should have left him dead at her feet.

The pieces fell together, and a slow grin tugged at Ashtead's mouth, only to fade again the next moment. Lydia must have been conversing with Jacoby when a literary gem intruded on his thoughts. The playwright would have forgotten her, forgotten his surroundings, forgotten everything as he became engulfed in his creation. And Lydia was not the female to be treated in such a manner. In short, she had taken snuff. Poor Lydia. He turned back toward Edwina, only to find himself facing Miss Fanny Marlowe.

The young lady grasped his hand. "Dance with me!" she commanded. "Please, or I shall be left with the most odious partner."

Ashtead glanced at Edwina, who studied her cards. He could hardly interrupt the game now that it had actually begun. Accepting the situation, he turned to Miss Marlowe with a bow. "You honor me."

Eddie forced her polite smile to remain in position as she faced Captain Kennilworth across the table. Ashtead had deserted her. How could he? He must have seen the plea for rescue in the look she had given him. One moment she had thought him on the verge of coming, the next he had been nowhere in sight. It might be foolish of her, but she felt betrayed.

Several people stood about them, watching, discussing

the progress of their game. She had to escape before—
She heard someone laying a wager on her taking the
next trick, and her heart sank. Nothing could do her
more harm. And nothing could make Kennilworth angrier, it seemed. His scowl grew more pronounced, and
the look he directed at her held pure venom.

Eddie pretended to yawn, then played her last few
cards. Behind her, someone called out her total for the
three hands they had played, and someone else reported
Kennilworth's lesser score. She cringed inwardly. It was
time she made her exit. Already the captain shuffled the
cards; she had to act quickly.

She rose. "I am sorry, Captain. I find I am too tired
to continue. Pray forgive me."

His eyes gleamed. "You would forfeit the game?"

"Willingly." She stifled another pretend yawn.

"Forfeit?" declared one of the onlookers. "No need
for that, Kennilworth. You've played three hands. Let it
stand, and be glad you did not play out the rest. She
would have beaten you handily."

"No," Eddie protested, but could not make herself
heard over the jocular comments of their audience. She
repeated her apologies to the captain, adding, "Why do
we not simply nullify the score, since I am unable to
complete the entire game?"

"Pray do not insult me. I pay my debts of honor," he
said through his teeth. He drew out a wad of flimsies
and cast several on the table before her.

"It was not my intention—" she began, but he rose,
directed a curt bow toward her, and stalked off.

She should never have allowed him to trap her into
this rematch. She had made him angrier; in fact, he be-
haved as if she had disgraced him before the watchers.
If only Ashtead had prevented them from beginning. He

could have. But he had chosen to ignore her pleading look. She wished she had never ventured forth from the house this night.

She moved away from the table, and found she no longer walked upon a carpet, but upon thick green grass, sprinkled liberally with poppies, hyacinths, bluebells, and daisies. A thick forest of elms and sycamores replaced the walls, and the lilting cries of robins, blackbirds, and willow warblers filled the air. Kings, queens, and knaves of every suit populated the tables, and in their hands they held dragonflies instead of cards. Lambs gamboled here and there amongst the players. Xanthe, it seemed, was trying to cheer her.

Jacoby, dressed as a shepherd, sat near the door. She greeted him, hoping for some kind word, but he did not seem to hear. Depressed, she reentered the ballroom and looked about for her fairy godmother. She found instead Lydia, who sat upon a chair in a corner, plying her fan with undue force. Eddie joined her, taking the seat at her side.

"Did you happen to see Sir William?" Lydia asked without looking up. The fan increased its pace.

"Yes. His new valet is to be congratulated."

Lydia sniffed. "I pity the poor female whom he will eventually marry. She will be invisible to him whenever he is writing. There is nothing worse than being ignored by one's husband."

"But he can be quite charming when one can capture his attention," Eddie pointed out.

"Yes, *when!*" came Lydia's savage response. "I suffered one marriage where I was ignored. That was quite enough. I want a husband who is *aware* of me, who will take action without having to be asked a dozen or more times. Oh, I would not mind caring for him when he is consumed by his plays, but oh! how I long for someone who would also take care of *me*."

The longing in Lydia's words echoed within Eddie. "Why must gentlemen be so vexatious?" Eddie demanded of her friend.

Lydia sighed. "You are lucky you escaped from an arranged marriage. From any marriage, I should say. Particularly," she added with feeling, "to my brother."

Eddie looked up at her quickly, surprised by the force of this sentiment. "What has he done to distress you?"

"He is as odious as the rest of his sex, without a thought or consideration for anyone but himself. I asked him to take me home because I have the most dreadful headache, but he refused, and simply because he wished to flirt with Miss Marlowe."

Eddie followed the direction of Lydia's glare, and was rewarded with the unwelcome sight of Ashtead waltzing with the young lady, their gazes locked upon one another. Her spirits sank even lower.

Lydia let out an exasperated sigh. "Let a gentleman be but good-looking, and females become the most foolish creatures in nature. You would not believe the number of caps that have been set at him, or the number of hearts he has broken."

"Hearts or hopes?" came Eddie's cynical response. "He is a matrimonial prize of the first water."

"Both, most like." Lydia glowered at her folded hands.

"I had gained the impression he did not fancy Miss Marlowe's company above half. Why—" She broke off, a sick sensation assailing her stomach. Miss Marlowe was a considerable heiress, and Ashtead needed money. "Her fortune for my grandfather's title? I suppose they would both consider it a good exchange. Is it not fortunate for him she has her heart set upon becoming a marchioness?"

And that was why he had left her to Kennilworth's revenge, so he could pursue a fortune. She had thought better of him than that. Indignation welled within her at his having thrown her to a wolf just so he could pursue his sordid purpose.

As she glared at him, he leaned closer to say something softly in his partner's ear; the young lady's giggling response made the flirtatious nature of the comment obvious. Eddie swelled with indignation for his callous treatment of both Lydia and herself. Then the music ended, and she had the dubious honor of seeing him kiss Miss Marlowe's hand before leading her from the floor.

Well, if he could not be troubled to take his poor, suffering sister home, perhaps Sir William Jacoby might be stirred from his literary withdrawal to perform this minor but immensely practical service.

She returned to the card room only to find his chair unoccupied. She looked about, vexed with him for unwittingly thwarting her attempt to boost him in Lydia's esteem. *Men,* she fumed, and had to fight back an irrational desire to burst into tears.

"What on earth possessed you to game with Kennilworth?" Ashtead's voice demanded from behind her. "I should have thought you'd show more sense than that."

She turned about, her outrage at so unjust an attack rendering her speechless. Every one of his iniquities sprang to her mind, tumbling over one another to be the first to leap from her tongue. After a moment, words she could not hold back escaped her. "I hadn't believed the stories about you—until now."

His eyes narrowed. "And which stories might those be?"

Her lip curled. "That you show neither taste nor discretion in your flirtations."

He stiffened, as if she had thrown a bucket of freezing water over him. "At least I have never been accused of a blatant want of conduct."

"Have you not?" she demanded. "What a shocking oversight on the part of the gossips. No, I cannot believe it possible. But have no fear. After this repugnant display of fortune hunting, I feel certain the problem will rectify itself."

About them, heads turned. She could feel the gazes upon them, for she had spoken louder than she had intended. Ashtead grasped her arm, probably to remove them to some isolated corner, but she pulled away, shaking off his grip, too angry to care. Through clenched teeth, in a voice that carried far too well, she said, "I can only be glad I had the good sense to run away rather than marry you."

A shocked giggle sounded from just behind them, and Ashtead's eyes flashed with fury. In a tone that dripped ice, he said, "I have no need of anyone's fortune. My great-uncle has signed the papers making me his exclusive heir. Which is just as well," he added, discretion and judgment evaporating, "for it allows me the freedom to tell you I wouldn't be tied to such a vixen as you for any consideration." With that, he turned on his heel and stalked off.

Ten

Xanthe hovered several inches above the sand, seated cross-legged on an elaborate carpet of reds and golds, woven after the Turkish fashion. Beside her hovered a bronze brazier, its coals glowing as it warmed the chill breeze that blew in from the ocean. Titus crouched before her, head low, just the tip of his tail twitching as he watched the angel fish that swam through the air. One toe jerked, then the massive feline pounced, only to find himself amidst a kaleidoscopic image, with multiple fragments of his former quarry now pursuing him. He settled on his considerable haunches and undertook the all-consuming occupation of smoothing one whisker back into position.

"Ashtead is far too accustomed to having his own way," Xanthe said. She hummed softly, and a delicate crystal glass of almond vanilla liqueur appeared in her hand. She swirled the amber liquid, then looked down at Titus. "Have you nothing to say?"

The feline paused and blinked.

"True. But one can understand how she feels. Since her parents died, no one has ever considered her wishes or feelings in the least. It is only natural she should long to be truly loved. Still, it is very frustrating."

She hummed a lively measure, and a miniature fire-breathing dragon hovered in the air. A princess in a long, flowing gown materialized before it. The tiny figure cowered a moment, then reached down and drew a gleaming sword from the sand and thrust at the dragon, who countered with his fiery breath. Their battle continued for several moments; then a knight in gleaming armor strode into the scene. With a sweep of one strong arm, he set the princess aside and took her place. Rather than retreating to safety, the princess turned her sword on the knight, and the two exchanged blows. The dragon sat back on its plump haunches, watching, a fiery chuckle escaping it.

Xanthe sighed. "They can keep up this farce indefinitely," she told Titus.

The cat emitted a series of noises that sounded like *eck, eck, eck.*

"Yes," Xanthe agreed. "It is too much to be hoped they will show any common sense. For their own sakes, I suppose we shall have to intervene."

The tip of Titus's tail twitched.

Xanthe laughed. "All right, for our sakes too."

She looked back to where her princess and knight still engaged in deadly combat. She hummed a bar, and an elderly man limped into the scene. The dragon reached out one lazy claw and pinned him to the sand. At once, the princess and knight abandoned their fight, turning as one to aid the newcomer, battling the dragon in perfect harmony with one another. The dragon let out a yelp and vanished. The elderly gentleman struggled to his feet and dusted off his armor, and the princess and her knight fell into one another's arms.

"Happy ending," Xanthe mused.

Titus's nose twitched, and he made a *myap* sound.

"Well," Xanthe said, considering, "perhaps you're

right. Call it the beginning of a far more enjoyable battle."

The cat stared at her, unblinking.

"How?" Xanthe tilted her head to one side, frowning. "Well, it is usually best if people reveal their true natures, is it not? So many humans spend so much effort trying to disguise who and what they really are, even from themselves. It is no wonder they are all so confused most of the time. Yes, I believe our players must be encouraged to behave in a manner true to their own characters. What?" She glanced at Titus, who regarded her fixedly. "No, I haven't the faintest notion what will happen. Is it not delightful? We shall be surprised as well."

Eddie rose early after a night of little sleep. The whole wretched scene with Ashtead haunted her, replaying itself over and over, each time becoming a little more terrible. It didn't seem possible she could have accused him of being a fortune hunter in front of so many people. She had thought it was he who suffered from an excess of explosive temper. And now she had been guilty—horribly so!—of the same folly.

But perhaps it was for the best. She had been on the verge of begging his pardon, of confessing regret at her unforgivable outburst, of seeking a return to the closeness she had come to welcome from him. But then he had spoken, and each of his words had made his true, unflattering opinion of her abundantly clear. She might never have otherwise known how truly little he valued her.

And there it was. He neither wanted nor needed her. He had his fortune; she didn't doubt for a moment he had spoken the truth about her grandfather's will. Which meant he had everything—and she had nothing that she did not earn herself. Well, she had known the old gentleman would never forgive her, never accept her back. So now she was truly on her own, for Ashtead would have nothing further to do with her either.

Depressed, she selected one of her Xanthe-supplied gowns at random. It floated over her head, fastened itself, then puffed out its tiny sleeves. She went to stand before the mirror, and as she watched, her hair arranged itself in a mass of ringlets. If only fairy magic could make the rest of life as easy. She descended the stairs, and found Xanthe already in the breakfast salon, drinking tea while half a dozen tiny fairies serenaded her on miniature instruments.

Eddie had barely finished her own first cup when Lydia bustled into the room. She dropped onto a chair and accepted the coffee Xanthe handed her. "I cannot stay, for I have promised to drive out with Aunt Hester. Only after last evening— And tonight we are to go to the concert . . ." Her voice trailed off.

"Do you mean that ridiculous quarrel?" Eddie waved it aside as if it had not, in fact, caused her a sleepless night and innumerable reproaches and regrets. "Have no fear. I know perfectly well that were we to cry off from attending in your brother's party, it would create just such a scandal as he would most detest. I am not one for so paltry a revenge, especially when much of the blame lies with me. No, I shall attend, and I shall behave in a civil manner."

Lydia regarded her in uncertainty. "You were both so very angry."

Eddie forced a laugh, realized it sounded dreadful, and tried to turn it into a cough. "Surely you are aware that Ashtead and I quarrel at the drop of a hat. I only regret that this time we showed the poor taste to conduct it in public. Did not your brother reassure you upon that head?"

Lydia looked at her shrewdly. "I have not seen him. He has not yet come downstairs this morning—if he even came home last night. I thought him uncommonly out of temper—even for him."

Warmth, from anger, from remembered pain, rose in Eddie's cheeks. "Then he probably spent the predawn hours drinking with one of his cronies. Now, let us talk of something that truly matters. How do little Anne and dear little Gregory go on? And are you truly leaving Brighton the day after tomorrow? Do they not want to remain?"

Lydia hesitated. "My plans are not quite settled," she said at last.

"Well, perhaps the concert tonight will induce you to remain. Do you know, I have never heard Madame Giovanetti sing," said Eddie.

"My poor love!" Lydia cried. "You have never heard anyone, have you?"

"Once," Eddie corrected. "When I was very small, Pappa took me to London. I fell asleep before it was over."

That made Lydia laugh, and eased the tension about her eyes. "Pray do not do so tonight," she begged, and took her leave.

The day passed, empty, devoid of pleasure. Not even Xanthe's magical surprises could lift Eddie's spirits. At last, though, the time came to dress for the evening, and she stood before her wardrobe, considering her gowns with more care than usual. She must see Ashtead, there could be no avoiding it. But his presence would have little to do with her, aside from the initial awkwardness when they first encountered one another. She would behave as if nothing had happened, as if neither of them had ever spoken harsh, unforgivable words. If he chose to be difficult or disagreeable, she would not descend to that level. She would be cool and civilized, for in truth, and despite the secret dreams she foolishly had built around him, they had never been more than the most casual of friends.

Her strength of will was put to the test as soon as they arrived, for he awaited them beside Mrs. Winslow just inside the entrance to the Old Ship, whose ballroom had been converted into a performance hall for the evening's concert. If he had spent the night in drunken debauchery, he showed no signs of it. He appeared as elegant as ever in his evening dress. More so, if possible. She looked away from the rough profile, with its squared chin and commanding brow, and ordered her heart to stop aching. It paid her no heed.

"There you are." Hester Winslow stepped forward, clasping Xanthe's hand. "Now, if dear Eddie's uncle will but arrive, our party will be complete."

Eddie greeted Mrs. Winslow, her smile held with considerable effort. Ashtead stood so close, yet he had not so much as glanced at her. "You have brought Sir William up to scratch then?"

Mrs. Winslow laughed. "He wished to question poor Lydia more closely upon the behavior of her children. I doubt he remembered he had any other purpose in coming here."

Eddie acknowledged the likelihood of this, then turned to meet the cold, forbidding stare of Ashtead. "We must thank you for your kind invitation," she managed without so much as a tremor in her voice.

He inclined his head. "I feel certain you will enjoy the performance."

The performance, yes. As for the rest of the evening spent in his company . . . No, it didn't bear thinking about. She allowed him to escort her to the group of seats he had reserved, but greeted with relief his excuse that he must return to the lobby to await the arrival of her uncle. To her surprise, Lydia sat there, very much alone.

Eddie took the chair at her friend's side. "Where is Sir William?"

"He has left." Lydia's voice sounded hollow, but resigned. "It seems that something I said provided him with just the idea he needed, and he determined not to waste a moment before committing it to paper."

Eddie clasped Lydia's hand for a moment, but could find nothing to say. Poor Lydia. Acquaintance with Jacoby had wrought quite a change in her, turning her thoughts toward another marriage. But what her friend wanted from Jacoby, that gentleman seemed incapable of giving.

About them, the audience moved to take seats, and the accompanist took his place at the pianoforte. Silence settled over the vast chamber, and the stately figure of the famed singer moved to the center of the makeshift stage. Ashtead ushered Mrs. Winslow and Xanthe into their places, then took the seat at the end of the row.

Eddie closed her eyes to allow the liquid soprano voice to wash through her. But one thought, one longing, kept interfering with the music. She wanted Ashtead at her side. Yet why she should long for his presence was beyond her. They never had anything pleasant or helpful to say to one another. And he had made it very clear last night that he didn't particularly like her. How could she ever have permitted herself to think she might care for him? And why must her confused emotions hurt so much?

For that matter, why should thoughts of him destroy this evening for her? She had never heard a voice so beautiful, or music so exquisitely suited to the woman who sang it. The performance should enthrall her. Instead she tried to glance across Xanthe and Mrs. Winslow in a casual manner for a glimpse of Ashtead, to see if he enjoyed it. She could not make out his face in the darkness, and that left her disconsolate.

She dragged her thoughts from him, back to the aria, then on to her purpose in having come to Brighton. She had almost won enough money to be independent. As soon as her time with Xanthe ended, she would move deep into the country and never have to see Ashtead again. Yet she would miss his family. Lydia, the sister she never had. Mrs. Winslow, a loving aunt. If Ashtead had wanted her, if he'd loved her, she could have gained a whole family as well.

Instead, she would be alone.

Well, she was used to that. This brief, magical interlude in her life would provide her with memories. She would learn to be content again on her own.

The last, high note hovered pure in the air, then faded. Silence filled the room; then applause broke out, raucous after the sweetness of the music. Madame Giovanetti retired to a back room, and the audience rose to seek refreshments from the tables that lined the back of the hall. Eddie opened eyes she had kept closed, surprised that so much time could have passed so quickly. She must try to win a little extra money so she might indulge herself with an occasional visit to a theater or concert.

She found Mrs. Winslow standing near the punch

bowl, sipping from her glass. When Eddie reached her side, the woman turned to her with a slight crease forming in her brow. "I do hope your uncle has not taken ill. He sounded so pleased at the prospect of this evening."

Eddie frowned. "He seemed quite well when I saw him earlier. Nor did he say anything about a change in his plans. I wonder what could have occurred to keep him away."

"Men!" declared Mrs. Winslow, with just the same force and loathing as either Lydia or Eddie herself might have used.

Eddie spent the remainder of the concert watching for her uncle's arrival, but he did not put in an appearance. Mrs. Winslow also kept glancing toward the door in a manner that grew more irritated as the evening drew on. When Madame Giovanetti had taken her last bow, Ashtead's aunt announced that she had developed the headache and desired to return to the house at the earliest possible moment.

Eddie too was relieved to be able to slip away into the night, away from the crowd, away from Ashtead. She bade Xanthe good night as soon as they arrived home, and made her way to her room to prepare for bed. She washed with the hot water that poured itself into her basin, held out her arms while her evening gown danced off her and her nightgown took its place, then slid between sheets at once. Sleep, though, took its time in coming.

It seemed she had barely achieved oblivion when, in the darkness of the early morning hours, a sound dragged her from her long-sought slumbers. She lay in her bed for a hazy moment, her brain puzzling out the odd tapping pattern, until she emerged sufficiently from her sleep-fogged state to identify it. Gravel, hitting her window. Curious, she threw off the covers and crossed the room to peer down through the shadowed fastness of the night.

She could just make out the huddled shape of a person crouching beside a shrub below. The face turned upward as the arm prepared to heave another missile, and the pale moonlight illumined the unmistakable features of her Uncle Marmaduke. She opened the window, waved to let him know she had seen him, then lit a candle and went to let him in.

She had descended to the lower floor before she woke sufficiently to wonder what could have brought him in so mysterious a fashion. Unease replaced her sleepiness, and she hurried to the front of the house. By the time she had dragged back the bolt and swung wide the door, questions filled her mind.

Marmaduke leaned forward to kiss her cheek, his manner somewhat distracted. "Sorry to wake you." He glanced over his shoulder, looking searchingly up and down the street, then pushed past her into the hall.

Her uneasiness took firm root. She too glanced up and down the street, then closed—and bolted—the door. "What's amiss?" she whispered as she steered him toward the salon. With the taper she carried, she ignited the wicks on a three-branched candelabrum.

He pressed her into a chair, but didn't take one himself. Instead he paced across the room, then back to stand before the hearth, in which only a few embers still glowed. "I'm leaving," he announced abruptly.

She waited, silent, knowing there would be more. He said nothing, though, merely standing there, his hands clasping and unclasping behind his back. What agony of mind distressed him? She had thought he might have formed an attachment to Hester Winslow. Had he? Had Mrs. Winslow rejected him? But it didn't seem like her uncle to take it like this. Eddie groped for any sign of change she had seen in him over the last few days, but could think of nothing except his absence from the concert this night. "You did not come to hear Madame Giovanetti sing," she said at last.

"No." He fell silent again.

"Where were you?" she tried. "We all missed you."

He drew a deep breath. "My dearest niece, I was behaving foolishly. Foolishly even by my standards."

She kept her voice light, gentle, not allowing the nervousness that filled her to sound in her words. "In what way?"

A deep sigh escaped him. "I agreed to what I thought would be a single game of piquet late in the afternoon." His voice sounded flat, devoid of his usual humor, devoid of any spark.

"And you lost." Still, he lost frequently. She didn't see where that would cause him to behave in so odd a manner.

He didn't seem to hear. "I must be the most wretched flat. I kept on playing to try to— But that's neither here nor there, since it didn't answer. The long and the short of it is I'm ruined." He drew a steadying breath. "But I must be off. I couldn't leave without seeing you, my dear. To have recovered you after so long, only to lose you again—" He shook his head. "You'll make my apologies to Mrs. Winslow for not saying my farewells in person, of course."

"But you cannot leave. If you owe your opponent money—"

"I cannot pay it," he said simply.

"But it is a debt of honor!"

His brow darkened as he regarded her. "A debt of *dis*honor, my dear."

She blinked at him. "How do you mean?"

He glowered at the coals. "I believe that his play was not entirely aboveboard."

She considered this. "He *cheated?*"

Marmaduke nodded. "I couldn't prove it, and that was my undoing. I kept trying to see how he did it. If I could have just discovered his trick, it would have canceled the debt, and I could have exposed him for the curst dog he is. But in the end, I lost. Utterly."

Eddie's mind raced, calculating. "Surely he will give you time to pay."

Uncle Marmaduke shook his head, his expression grim. "I am, at this moment, fleeing a debtor's prison."

"A— He cannot!" cried Eddie. "Why would any-one—" She broke off abruptly. This was all too smoky by half, as her father used to say. Why would anyone lure Uncle Marmaduke into a game and then cheat? All the world knew he hadn't a feather to fly with. And why would anyone demand instant repayment, under threat of a debtor's prison? It was unheard of! But Uncle Mar-maduke took it seriously enough to flee the country. She fixed her erratic relative with a steady, compelling gaze. "With whom did you play?"

He cleared his throat. "A man—I will not distinguish him by calling him a gentleman—whom it would be best for you to avoid completely in the future, my dear. He means us ill."

"Who?" she insisted.

"Captain Kennilworth."

She digested this. "It is because of me, is it not?" she said slowly. "Because I embarrassed him by defeat-ing him in front of his friends. Isn't it?" she demanded.

Marmaduke straightened. "This has nothing to do with you. It is I who lost the money, not you."

"But he told you that you could apply to me for the monies you need to pay the debt, did he not?"

"I won't do it." Uncle Marmaduke turned to face her once more. "I may have hung on your pappa's sleeve while he was alive, but I'm not about to break the shins of his only daughter. No, my dear. I will not touch a penny of your winnings."

"Oh, yes you will," she breathed. "He played with you in order to take a revenge on me, and I'll not have you suffer for it. How much did you lose?"

"No," he said simply.

She rose, arms akimbo, and faced him. "Do you think the money is more important to me than you are? And only consider. I have won it all over the course of the last few weeks. I can win it again. Now do not be absurd, Dearest Uncle. A portion of it was Kennilworth's at one time, after all. Once he knows I have been the one who has had to part with the money, he will have had his revenge. And then he will be satisfied and leave us alone. Believe me, it will be worth any price to be free of the man."

"I don't like this," muttered Marmaduke.

She smiled. "I know you don't. But I don't mind, truly I don't. And how can you bring yourself about if you languish in a debtor's prison? No, let me give you the money; then I will set about winning more. How much?" He still hesitated, and she added with some force, "If you will not tell me, I will be forced to go to him in the morning and give it to him myself, which will grant him far too much satisfaction, not to mention dealing a mortifying blow to my pride. So let us have no more arguing. How much do you need?"

"Just over eight thousand pounds," came his reluctant response.

"Eight—" She bit back her exclamation. "Wait here," she said when she had mastered her voice.

She hurried from the room, refusing to allow herself to think, to consider. She had the amount. In fact, she had won eight thousand four hundred pounds. She had almost reached her hard-earned independence. And now—

No, she could not allow Uncle Marmaduke to be clapped in irons over a debt that owed its roots to cheating, to Kennilworth's revenge against her. The captain had calculated it nicely, knowing her weak point, that she would do anything for her beloved uncle.

She reached her chamber, and drew the packets of flimsies, wrapped neatly in several of her embroidered handkerchiefs, from their various hiding places. Eight thousand, plus one hundred pounds. She hurried from the room and returned to find her uncle in the hall, his hand on the front door.

"You are not leaving without these!" she exclaimed.

He turned, his expression haggard. "My dearest niece—"

She thrust the packets into his reluctant hands. "Deposit these with a bank, then write him a draft upon it. I do not trust him."

Marmaduke nodded, glum.

"This is *my* war with Kennilworth," she reminded him. "You should never have been drawn into it."

"He probably could not have cheated against you," came Marmaduke's sober response. "You only play where there are any number of people about."

"How did he induce you to play in the first place?" she inquired.

Marmaduke glowered, but made no response.

"Did he threaten me?" she hazarded.

Marmaduke flushed. "He's a scoundrel."

"Pay him off. Then we will neither of us ever have dealings with him again." She pushed her uncle out into the early dawn and closed the door firmly behind him. She leaned back against it, her knees suddenly too weak to support her.

Eight thousand pounds. It had taken her six weeks to accumulate it, innumerable hands of piquet, a staggering number of opponents. And she only had two weeks remaining in her agreement with Xanthe.

She could never recoup so tremendous a sum. But neither could she allow her beloved uncle to languish in prison. Slowly she slid down the length of the door until she sat huddled on the floor, her arms cradling her knees. She could not return to her grandfather, Ashtead did not want her, she had no claim on Xanthe beyond the next two weeks.

In short, she had no money, nowhere to go, and no hope.

Eleven

Sleep did not return to Eddie that night. She tossed restlessly in her bed, her thoughts racing, trying to hit upon some scheme to save herself from this disaster. And it didn't help at all that she suffered from an overwhelming desire to run to Ashtead and seek comfort from him. She closed her eyes tight, trying to concentrate on Uncle Marmaduke, on knowing she had done the right thing. Yet in her mind's eye, her uncle's rounded chin turned to Ashtead's squared one, his unruly shock of gray hair turned to Ashtead's wind-blown dark brown waves. Why must Ashtead haunt her thoughts, haunt her heart?

Because she loved him. The answer erupted into her consciousness, definite and devastating. She loved him, and had done so for a very long while. His drinking, his flirting, his outrageous behavior—none of it mattered, for she recognized it as the restless outlet of one who sought his heart's desire, but could not find it.

Her fingers plucked at the coverlet as she contemplated this unwelcome realization. She loved him. She acknowledged that for an incontrovertible fact. But it changed nothing. Or perhaps it made everything worse. Now, instead of merely knowing she had thrown away her chance to achieve her wish, she could also know she had no chance of winning the heart of the one man who would always possess hers.

But thinking about him did her no good. She had to concentrate on her future, and so far she could only think of what she could *not* do. Ashtead, her grandfather, Xanthe—she had no claim on any of them, could not hang upon their sleeves. She had to fend for herself.

And it was all her own fault. She had allowed her temper to rule her. She had said and done things for which she could not be forgiven, even defied her own sound judgment by playing against Kennilworth. She had no one to blame but herself for her predicament.

Of course, Kennilworth had taken his revenge upon her by cheating. She rolled over, burying her face in her pillow. Had he deprived her of her competence by fair means, it would have been easier to accept. But to be cheated out of it—

She sat up, her mind abruptly racing as her fingers absently smoothed her muslin pillowcase. Kennilworth had no right to her hard-earned money. He had no right to make poor Uncle Marmaduke feel miserable and guilty. He had cheated. She would find a way to make him pay it back, and then she and Uncle Marmaduke could be comfortable again. Ruthlessly she blocked the sudden longing that she might be able to make things right with Ashtead as well. That was beyond her ability to fix. But Kennilworth was another matter.

She would hold a card party, and Kennilworth would be her guest of honor. She would play against him under conditions where he could not cheat. But where? She and Xanthe could not entertain such a gentleman at their house. Perhaps if Uncle Marmaduke acted as her host— No, Kennilworth would scent a trap and refuse her invitation.

With a groan, she sank her head into her hands. The party would have to be held by some gentleman, and one Kennilworth would not suspect of any duplicity. Wretchedly, she considered each of her recent opponents, but not one of them did she know well enough to approach with so delicate and outrageous a request.

Only a day or so ago, she could have asked Ashtead. That would have been ideal, for with Mrs. Winslow to play hostess for him, Eddie could have attended the "party" with impunity. Only she could not ask Ashtead.

But did she have to?

The idea was so reprehensible, yet so perfect . . .

Ashtead and Mrs. Winslow *could* hold the party, if Ashtead knew nothing about it.

She sank back against the pillows, working out the details.

Potential problems began to occur to her in the early morning light. How could she assure that Ashtead did *not* know? How could she prevent Kennilworth from cheating? Would he even accept an invitation from Ashtead? Would Mrs. Winslow go along with this shocking plan—without telling her nephew?

She had to try. This represented her only chance for a future. It had to work. She would *make* it work.

Bleary-eyed and strained, she selected a gown at random and dragged herself down the stairs to fortify herself with breakfast. Titus greeted her at the door of the sunny parlor, rubbing against her ankles, an unusually warm greeting from the independent feline. She scooped him up in her arms and, to the accompaniment of his loud purrs, carried him into the breakfast salon.

This morning, Xanthe entertained herself with a line

of opera dancing hippopotami wearing short ruffled skirts of net and an array of ostrich plumes on their heads. The fairy sat back from the table, a cup of tea in one hand, conducting the festivities by waving her fork like a baton. Eddie could muster no more than a faint smile in response, and made her way to the sideboard, where she proceeded to select a number of herrings for Titus's delectation.

Xanthe cut the hippopotami off in mid-pirouette. "You won't regret giving the money to your uncle, my love."

Eddie turned to face her. Even after living with the fairy for so many weeks, Xanthe's ability to know all that went on—or all that one even contemplated—still amazed her. She drew a shaky breath. "Won't I?"

Xanthe smiled. "My love, could you have lived with yourself had you acted otherwise?"

"No." Eddie regarded the chafing dish filled with coddled eggs, and found she had no appetite. She settled at the table with only a cup of tea. "You know what I am planning." She made it a statement.

Xanthe's mischievous violet eyes flashed with amusement. "An inspired plan, my love."

Eddie set down her cup, staring intently at her fairy godmother. "Will it succeed?"

"That is up to you." Xanthe leaned back in her chair. "You have my aid, you know that. But in the end, your success or failure lies in your own hands."

Eddie nodded. "Will you come with me this morning?"

Xanthe shook her head. "You will have no need of me. Ashtead will have gone out just before you arrive, you may count on me for that. You may speak to his aunt and sister in private. But if I am there, you might be tempted to rely too much upon me."

Eddie sipped her tea, feeling somewhat better. When she rose at last to take her departure, she stooped to kiss her godmother's cheek. "Thank you," she said softly, and went to face her preparations.

She arrived to find the ladies still drinking their own tea in the breakfast parlor, discussing the previous evening's concert. Ashtead, she noted with mixed satisfaction and regret, was not present, just as Xanthe had promised. Dear Xanthe. Perhaps Eddie just might win through yet, with the fairy's humming to support her.

"A most beautiful voice," declared Mrs. Winslow in subdued tones when Eddie had taken a seat.

"All in all, a delightful evening," agreed Lydia. Her smile seemed somewhat wan.

"Indeed it was." Eddie could not keep the dry note from her voice. Sir William's obliviousness hurt Lydia, and strange as it might seem, Uncle Marmaduke's absence from the festivities had dampened Mrs. Winslow's spirits. Gentlemen, Eddie reflected, caused everyone a great deal of pain and trouble.

The footman withdrew from the room, and Eddie set her cup back on its saucer. "I have come for a specific purpose," she announced. "I need your help."

Lydia looked up, drawn from her cocoon of unhappiness. "Of course."

"We should be delighted," agreed Mrs. Winslow.

"You might not be." Eddie hesitated, then plunged ahead. "It is a terrible imposition, and I know it, but I cannot think of any other way to carry the day."

Both ladies watched her expectantly, albeit with a touch of unease on Mrs. Winslow's part. "Cannot your godmamma—" that lady began, then broke off. "No, how silly of me. If she could have helped, you would have gone to her. Tell us, my love."

"It is Captain Kennilworth." In as few words as possible, she explained the situation.

"It is beyond anything!" cried Lydia when Eddie had finished. "Of course you must teach him a lesson."

"Quite horrid," agreed Mrs. Winslow, though with some reserve. "But— Oh, my dear, I hate to speak ill of one who is your close relative, but I cannot understand how Mr. Rutland could ever have placed you in so dreadful a fix."

"It is not his fault," Eddie repeated, anxious to reassure Mrs. Winslow on this point. It seemed to be Uncle Marmaduke's role in this little drama that distressed the woman the most. "Captain Kennilworth cheated, and Uncle Marmaduke sought to discover the means. Only the captain proved too deft for him."

Mrs. Winslow looked down at her hands folded about her teacup. "If Mr. Rutland were not a gamester, if he thought before he acted, if he cared for anyone or anything other than his own pleasure—" Her indignation swelled, cutting off her flow of words.

"Captain Kennilworth trapped him," Eddie insisted. "It was his desire for revenge against me that caused the trouble. And I will not let him succeed. I must win back my competence from him."

"Of course you must!" declared Lydia.

"Yes," agreed Mrs. Winslow. "But it will be best if we tell Ashtead, and allow him to deal with the captain."

"Absolutely not!" cried Eddie. "Why, what could Ashtead do? We have no absolute proof of the captain's cheating. So far, at least. Ashtead would most likely advise me to let the matter drop and have nothing further to do with the man. And that is something I cannot and will not do. I will not allow him to get away with what he has done."

Lydia nodded. "All men are marplots. I, for one, understand perfectly your desire to deal with the matter without any masculine interference."

"Well, as to that, I rather thought we should have my Uncle Marmaduke present," Eddie admitted. "If Captain Kennilworth becomes unpleasant, I would rather have someone here to help us. Besides, I need someone who knows piquet intimately to watch the play to assure that he does not cheat."

"But Mr. Rutland could not detect the cheating last evening," pointed out Mrs. Winslow.

"But this time he will sit beside Kennilworth and watch his handling of the cards." Eddie leaned forward, earnest. "From that position, there will be little the captain can do that cannot be seen. And Uncle Marmaduke," she added as the clincher, "will deal."

"It might work." Lydia looked to her aunt, whose features remained fixed in a thoughtful frown.

"There is one problem," Eddie went on. "We must make certain Ashtead learns nothing of the matter."

Lydia, then Mrs. Winslow, nodded in slow agreement. All three fell silent, considering.

"Perhaps we could send him off to have dinner with one of his friends," Lydia suggested.

"Provided one invited him," Eddie said. She propped one elbow on the table and sank her chin into her hand.

"And even then he might return too early," Mrs. Winslow pointed out.

Again, silence filled the room.

"We must get him out of Brighton," decided Lydia.

Mrs. Winslow looked up, hopeful. "How?"

"I could ask him to go to the Court for me," Lydia said thoughtfully.

"But you told him this morning you intend to return

there tomorrow," Mrs. Winslow reminded her. "He would insist upon waiting and escorting you."

"And he would probably suggest I ask Bentley to look over anything that worried me," Lydia agreed, disheartened.

"What of his own home?" Eddie looked from one to the other of her companions.

Lydia shook her head. "I have never known an estate to run as smoothly as his. Mr. Bentley inspects it upon occasion, as it is part of the Shoreham properties, but Ashtead always has everything running exactly as it ought."

Silence reigned again. Eddie sipped her tea, frowning, turning over various possibilities in her mind. "Ashtead is very managing, is he not?" she mused.

Lydia looked up. "Have you an idea?"

Eddie nodded slowly. "If he thought I were about to purchase a property, he might be induced to inspect it, might he not?"

Lydia clasped her hands. "It is the very thing! You must ask him as soon as he returns."

Eddie forced a smile she was far from feeling. "I fear we are not upon terms at the moment. It would be better if you approached him. You may say I told you about a cottage, but you have misgivings and would feel better if he looked it over before I could commit myself to some dreadful error."

Mrs. Winslow actually smiled through her troubles. "He will not be able to resist. Dear Ashtead, so very noble."

"And so very meddling," agreed Lydia.

This solution reached, they set about composing a note of invitation for Captain Kennilworth, to which they would affix Ashtead's name. This involved some little discussion before they reached a final wording, but at last Lydia copied it out in her fair hand. The others gathered about to read the final result.

"Do you think it wise to state that each guest is required to bring ten thousand pounds?" Mrs. Winslow asked.

"It is what will assure his attendance," Lydia said, not looking up from the note she studied.

"He will bring the sum because he will never think to lose it," Eddie agreed. "And with the prospect of so rich an evening of play, he will not be able to resist."

"And you are quite certain your uncle can prevent him from cheating?" Mrs. Winslow looked from Eddie to Lydia. "I do feel we ought to have Ashtead present, just to assure that all goes as you would wish."

"He would never permit us to carry this out!" cried Eddie. "Pray, promise you will say not a word to him."

"We will have Mr. Rutland," Lydia added.

Mrs. Winslow shook her head. "At least Sir William—"

The sadness returned to Lydia's eyes. "What possible help could he be? You may be certain some word or action would make him think of his play, and then he would forget all else and be completely useless to us. No, we have no need of any gentleman other than Eddie's uncle. We shall do perfectly well. And Eddie will have her chance to win back her competence."

Leaving Lydia to deal with her brother as soon as he returned, Eddie made her way home. There she paced the salon until she suddenly realized that a human-sized dragon paced right behind her on its hind legs, its front claws clasped behind its scaly back. It let out a fiery sigh every third or fourth step. Eddie looked reproachfully at Xanthe, who pored over a musical score beside the window.

"You are somewhat restless," the fairy pointed out with a touch of apology in her voice.

"I'm sorry." Eddie sank into a chair, and Titus sprang into her lap, circled, then settled down to purr. Her fingers stroked his thick fur. "It will be all right, will it not?"

Xanthe smiled. "My love, how can I possibly tell you the outcome in advance? My words might influence your behavior, and then all would turn out differently. Rest assured I will grant you the best opportunity to achieve the wish of your heart."

Eddie nodded, though her misgivings lingered. What, in truth, *was* the wish of her heart? Her independence, of course. But if she were honest— No, it did her no good. Xanthe did not meddle in love. It had its own magic, the fairy had said. And if Ashtead preferred beautiful, witty, worldly-wise heiresses, she could hardly beg her godmother to change the focus of his heart. She had best concentrate on the opportunity to win a competence granted her by Xanthe.

And she would not allow herself to consider the possibility of failure.

They were just sitting down to a light nuncheon for which Eddie had no appetite when the knocker sounded on the front door. A minute later, the footman showed Lydia into the room. She stood just over the threshold, her face flushed and eager, until the man closed the door behind her.

She moved forward in a rush. "Ashtead has just departed!"

Xanthe waved her toward a chair. "Join us, my dear."

Lydia cast off her bonnet and took a seat, her eyes

sparkling. "He returned just over an hour ago with— with Sir William. I told him you had formed the intention of purchasing this property in a village some thirty miles along the coast, and I feared you would take the word of this person and buy it without even seeing it." She cast a sideways glance at Eddie. "You would have been quite flattered to see how quickly he set about preparing for the journey."

"What, flattered to see how little faith he has in my judgment that he feels he must set forth at once?"

Lydia blinked at her. "But he was quite worried!"

"Which is exactly what you wanted, my love," Xanthe pointed out, a quaver of amusement in her voice.

"Yes," agreed Eddie, somewhat dully. "Of course. And he cannot possibly return until tomorrow. Well done, Lydia. Now, we must send our note to Captain Kennilworth."

"I have already done so." Lydia extracted a folded slip of paper from her reticule and held it out. "Here is his acceptance."

Eddie took it, scanned the scrawl, and her fingers tightened on the sheet. "Now," she said, "we must send for Uncle Marmaduke."

Eddie spent the remainder of the afternoon reviewing their plans. She could count on nothing, she knew. It could all fall apart so easily. Luck might not favor her, and Kennilworth had proved himself to be a shrewd player even without cheating. She might, in fact, lose money she no longer possessed.

And as for Ashtead's dashing off like that— She didn't know whether to be gratified that he took such concern in her welfare, or angered that he showed so little trust in her judgment. He probably acted out of a sense of duty. Once he saw her safely established, he would no longer need to feel guilt over her running away from her grandfather. With a clear conscience, he could wash his hands of her.

Depressed, she returned to her contemplation of the evening ahead. It began to loom as a misconceived and ill-fated adventure, as folly pure and simple. Ashtead would be quite right in his undoubted condemnation of it. Yet try as she might, she could think of no other scheme to bring herself about.

She could, of course, declare herself a gamestress, perhaps even open one of those discreet little houses in London that Uncle Marmaduke spoke of with such fondness. But she would not enjoy such a life. Nor, she told herself with considerable force, could she ever have been happy as the wife of Ashtead—or any other gentleman. She wanted to be her own mistress, to be ordered about by no one but herself.

She made her way to her chamber to select her gown for the night. At last, with Xanthe's amused magical help, she settled on a gauze robe of sea-foam green with tiny puff sleeves and a low décolletage discreetly filled with lace. A single ruffle adorned the hem, causing the skirts to sway gently as she walked. It was enough to give her sagging confidence a much-needed boost. If only Kennilworth could be distracted by her charms. But she doubted he would care for anything besides the chance to win even more money from her.

Xanthe stood back at last. "Perfect, my love." She hummed softly, then turned Eddie to the cheval glass to admire the sea-green ribands and lace that now threaded around the knot of her hair and through the thick ringlets.

"I made the wrong wish," Eddie said in an attempt

at lightness. "I should have asked for your abilities as a dresser."

Xanthe laughed. "Do not worry so, my love. Have faith in your abilities. And in your friends."

Eddie turned to face her. "That sounded like a pointed message."

Xanthe smiled. "True independence can be very lonely."

"I don't want to close people away from me," Eddie assured her. "I just don't want to be subject to their whims."

"We all are, my love, whether we realize it or not." Xanthe leaned forward and kissed her forehead. "Now, it is time for you to leave. Titus and I will be with you, watching in my basin."

Eddie regarded her in dismay. "You won't come?"

"You are independent, are you not?" Xanthe smiled. "Have confidence in yourself. But also know that I am here, humming. Now, go."

Not in the least reassured, Eddie made her way down the stairs. She wrapped a woolen shawl about her shoulders against the chill of the breeze blowing off the ocean, and made her way down the street to Hester Winslow's front porch. The door opened to her almost as soon as she knocked, and Edgarth let her into the hall. He took her shawl, then escorted her into the salon, where Lydia and Mrs. Winslow sat clutching glasses of ratafia.

Lydia sprang to her feet at once to pour Eddie a drink. "To brace our nerves," she said with an unsteady laugh.

A knock sounded on the front door, and Eddie tensed. But it was Uncle Marmaduke's familiar, if somewhat subdued, voice that responded to Edgarth, and in another moment his large, comforting shape filled the doorway. Lydia greeted him warmly.

Eddie ran to him. "I am so very glad you are here. You can have no idea how worried we are. Did you bring the cards?"

"In the hall." He pressed her hands. "And you know I will do my poor best this night."

"See that you do," ordered Mrs. Winslow in forbidding tones.

He turned to his hostess. "You blame me. But not possibly more than I blame myself."

"Nonsense," said Eddie quickly. "It was me he wished to take revenge upon, and he laid a cunning trap no one could have avoided. It is my fault completely for choosing to win my independence by playing cards."

"I think it was very brave of you," said Lydia. "And how could anyone guess Captain Kennilworth could be such a—such a scoundrel."

Edgarth entered then and announced dinner. Marmaduke turned to Hester Winslow and offered his arm. The woman hesitated, then accepted it without meeting his gaze. She took her place at the head of the table, with Lydia at the foot and Eddie and Uncle Marmaduke on either side. They could not, Eddie reflected, be accused of being a lively group this night.

The butler served slices of fish floating in a cream sauce, and the party's solemnity faded under Marmaduke's instant and vociferous approval. This led to a discussion with Mrs. Winslow on the merits of various types of fish, and which sauces best enhanced the flavor of each. The arrival of a duckling in an orange glacé, tiny peas adorned with sprigs of mint, and potatoes layered with wine-laced cheese brought an exclamation of satisfaction from the old gentleman, and the constraint of the evening vanished.

For them, at least. Eddie toyed with her portion, unable to swallow more than a morsel of each succeeding dish. By the time the footman removed a succulent rack of lamb from the table, and the butler replaced it with a confection of spun sugar and fairy cakes, she had given up even trying.

Lydia reached across, just touching her arm. "You will do splendidly," she assured Eddie. "Just as you always do. Even Ashtead says he has never encountered a finer player than you, and coming from him, that is high praise indeed."

Eddie managed a ghost of a smile. "But what if we cannot prevent Captain Kennilworth from cheating? What if—"

She broke off as the sounds of an arrival drifted into the room. Had Kennilworth come so soon? The door swung wide, and she looked up to see Ashtead filling the entry, his face a cold mask of anger, his clothing liberally spattered with mud.

"You will oblige me," he said through clenched teeth, "by explaining what the devil you meant by sending us off on a wild-goose chase."

Lydia paled. "I—" She broke off, finding nothing to say.

Ashtead advanced into the room, his gaze not on his sister but on Eddie. Behind him, Jacoby leaned against the doorjamb, his expression amiable but perplexed.

"Why do you not put off your dirt and join us for dinner," suggest Mrs. Winslow in a calm, authoritative voice.

"The devil with your dinner, madam," snapped

Ashtead. "Eddie, you will tell me what you are about. Now."

"No—nothing," she managed. A chill seeped into the pit of her stomach, leaving her weak. In all the catastrophes she had envisioned for the evening, Ashtead's return had not played a role. But if he found out, if he forbade the proceedings, if he refused to admit Kennilworth to the house, she would be utterly ruined.

"Did you not find the cottage?" Lydia tried.

"I had thought you meant to spend the night in the village," Mrs. Winslow added.

"And what do you mean by inspecting a cottage *I* mean to purchase?" Eddie demanded, recovering her wits and going on the offensive. *"I* never asked for your opinion."

"No," he said, his cold gaze steady on her face. "You did not. Because there is no cottage in that village, is there?"

"Of course there is!" Lydia declared.

"Any number of them, I should think," said Jacoby. "Only not a single one that fit your description was for sale."

Lydia's brow wrinkled. "There must have been a mistake. Surely—"

"You never could lie convincingly, Lydia. I don't know why I fell for it this morning," Ashtead snapped. "You may apologize to me later. Now, I want to know what harebrained scheme the four of you have concocted that required my absence."

Marmaduke, his mouth full of rum-flavored cake, nodded. "Shrewd head," he said when he could speak again. "Always knew you for a knowing one."

"Thank you," said Ashtead dryly. He looked around the table. "Aunt? Lydia? Eddie?" He settled on Eddie.

"You will come with me, if you please, and we will discuss this matter."

"There is nothing to discuss." Despite her best efforts, Eddie's voice trembled.

"Never did understand why they wouldn't tell you," Marmaduke put in. "Thought you'd get a rare kick out of it myself."

"Uncle!" protested Eddie.

Ashtead nodded. "Now," he said softly to Eddie, but his voice brooked no opposition. He took her by the elbow and drew her, protesting, from her chair.

"That's the ticket," said Marmaduke. "You run along with him and fix it up so he and Jacoby here can take their parts."

Eddie found herself propelled out of the dining room and across the hall, but before Ashtead could drag open the door to the salon, a knock once more sounded from the street. Eddie pushed her way into the salon, trying to drag Ashtead within, but she could not budge him. He waited, still holding her by the elbow, while the footman emerged from the back of the house and admitted Kennilworth.

The captain crossed the threshold, beaming. "I see I am not the first to arrive. Excellent, excellent. Splendid notion for a party, Ashtead."

"I am glad you think so." Nothing in Ashtead's tone betrayed his emotions. Only his grip on Eddie's arm tightened.

Mrs. Winslow burst out of the dining room. "My dear captain," she declared, taking his arm. "Do come into the drawing room and have a glass of wine. Ashtead will rejoin us in just a moment." She drew the captain away, throwing a frantic look over her shoulder at Eddie.

As soon as the two had vanished into the other room,

Ashtead propelled Eddie further into the salon. He released her but stood before the door, blocking her escape. "What crackbrained notion have you taken into your head?" he demanded. "What the devil is that Captain Sharp doing here?"

Eddie squared her shoulders and faced him. "This has nothing to do with you."

"Since your guest seems to think this is my party, I believe it does."

She considered that, but could find no valid argument against his reasoning.

The harshness in his face softened. "Why won't you tell me, Eddie?"

"Because this is *my* affair. I won't be thwarted by someone to whom it makes no difference."

"And what makes you think I will thwart you?"

There was nothing for it, she supposed. Her shoulders drooped and she turned away. "He entrapped poor Uncle Marmaduke into gaming with him, only he cheated, and then threatened Uncle with a debtor's prison if he did not pay him back. And I am not going to let him get away with it."

Ashtead listened in silence while she filled in more details, his brow growing darker and darker. When she finished, he paced away, hands behind his back, then spun to glare at her. "How dared your uncle put you in this position?"

"It was not his fault!" she protested.

"And how dared my aunt and sister not tell me what you planned. Have you not considered the possibility he might be dangerous if cornered? Do you honestly think you can force him to lose a fortune to you? You damned little fool, how dared you not trust me?"

In his face, she read the utter condemnation that she

had dreaded. She had been right in her estimation of his reaction, but that fact afforded her no satisfaction whatsoever. She had committed the sin of not confiding in him, and in his eyes, that was more unforgivable than any of the rest.

Twelve

The door opened, and Kennilworth strode in. "What's toward, Ashtead?" he demanded. "I understood there should be many players this night, yet there is only the one table in there. And here's your aunt going on about only two playing at a time."

Ashtead fixed Eddie with a meaningful glare, then turned to the captain. "My dear Kennilworth," he said, taking the man by the elbow in a manner that caused alarm to flicker across the captain's face. "How very good of you to accept my invitation. It seems there are surprises in store for us all this night."

Eddie winced at the anger latent in his words.

"What is the meaning of this?" Kennilworth repeated.

"A contest," said Ashtead, sweeping the man inexorably back to the drawing room. "A fair contest."

Kennilworth pulled away. "What the devil do you mean to imply by that?"

"Merely that you have nothing to fear. Lady Edwina wishes to pit her skill against a worthy opponent in a private way that will not engender any unseemly gossip. Eddie?" The sparkle of anger in his eyes belied the calmness of his voice.

Eddie stepped forward.

Mrs. Winslow moved to her side, clasping her hands.

"Good luck, my dear. Do not let that hardheaded nephew of mine put you off your game."

"You won't stay?" Panic surged through Eddie at the thought of losing one of her supporters.

"You will do very well without me." Mrs. Winslow leaned forward, kissed Eddie's cheek, then exited the chamber, leaving behind her the faint but comforting scents of lavender and rose.

The warmth behind the gesture tugged at Eddie. But now was not the time to regret the impending loss of such loving, comforting people in her life.

They had set the stage with care, with one small table for two, surrounded by chairs for the others to act as audience. No wonder the sight of it had raised Kennilworth's suspicions. Eddie moved past Ashtead without allowing herself to look at him, and seated herself. Her palms felt damp, and there was a distressing tightness in her breath.

Marmaduke strolled into the room, a medium-sized paper-wrapped parcel under one arm. "Evening, Kennilworth," he said cheerfully.

The man started, his widening eyes roaming from his erstwhile opponent to Ashtead. Marmaduke placed the package on the card table and unwrapped it, revealing thirty-six new packs of cards, enough for a fresh deck for each of the hands for six games. These he set to one side in neat stacks. "Quite new," he announced with pride. "Still have the seals on 'em."

Kennilworth's gaze darted around the room. He pulled his arm free from Ashtead's slackened grip and backed toward the door.

"Evening, Kennilworth." Jacoby leaned against the jamb in a not-quite negligent manner, effectively blocking any retreat from the room.

"You came here to game for high stakes, did you not? And you have here any number of witnesses to assure fair play." Marmaduke beamed at him. "The perfect setting, you might say."

"Indeed." Kennilworth recovered. "What a charming arrangement." He flashed a smile that was all teeth; not an ounce of warmth reached his eyes. With a flourish, he pulled out the chair opposite Eddie. "You cannot imagine how I look forward to this."

"Oh, I rather think we all can." Ashtead's smile showed as insincere as the captain's.

Lydia, Ashtead, and Uncle Marmaduke took the surrounding chairs, drawing them close to the table. Kennilworth reached for the first pack, but Marmaduke stopped him with a flamboyant gesture. He picked it up, held it out for the captain's inspection, then broke the seal and sorted out the lower pips. Eddie's fingers clenched together as she watched.

"Shall we begin with ten-pound points?" suggested Ashtead.

Inwardly, Eddie cringed at so great a sum, but she dared not protest. She had so little money left, the captain knew how to play, luck could be so fickle . . . The litany of fears that had hounded her throughout the day screamed once more in her mind. But she could not let herself think about them or she would freeze, be unable to play at all. Already, the cards began to pile up before her as Marmaduke dealt them out.

Lydia stirred in her seat, and Eddie cast her a wan smile. Lydia nodded encouragement, her gaze holding so much warmth and confidence that emotion welled in Eddie's throat. Uncle Marmaduke too watched her with a satisfied expression in his eyes that bespoke a faith in her skill she could not share at this moment.

She reached for her cards, only to pause. For her future, she reminded herself. She *could* do this. She had to. She picked them up and sorted them with a growing sense of dismay. She hadn't realized how much she'd hoped— But Xanthe stayed out of this. She held an ordinary hand, nothing more, nothing marvelous and guaranteed to let her win. It truly was up to her and her abilities.

But she held a sufficient variety of cards to feel fairly certain that Kennilworth's hand could be no better. She could feel his intensity, his concentration as he selected his discards. It suffocated her. She glanced toward Uncle Marmaduke, who leaned forward, concentrating on the captain. Ashtead too never took his gaze from the man. By the door, Jacoby still leaned negligently against the wall, not leaving his self-appointed post. Nor, she noted with a touch of surprise, did that dreamy expression creep over his countenance. For once, he paid attention.

They would not desert her, these friends of hers. Her heart swelled. Yes, she wanted to be independent, to make her own decisions. But she also wanted to share her life with these people, and she wanted them to know she did so by choice, not because she could not meet her own debts. She wanted them to know she needed them from love, not necessity.

She turned back to her cards and made her first play. Within moments she lost herself in the familiar pattern of calculating her opponent's strategy, what he must hold in his hand. She was actually surprised when she laid down her last card and took the trick.

Lydia, who held a pad of paper on which she had been tallying the scores, looked up. "That places you ahead by seventeen points, Eddie."

"A new deck?" Ashtead raised his eyebrows toward Marmaduke. That gentleman selected another pack, offered it to Kennilworth, who irritably waved it aside, not bothering to inspect the seal. Ashtead collected the cards from the table while Marmaduke prepared the new deck and dealt.

The play continued through the remaining five hands of the game, with fortunes shifting, favoring first one, then the other of them, until Eddie again took the last trick. A laugh of delight escaped Lydia. "You are Rubiconed, Captain Kennilworth."

The captain's face flushed. "Impossible!" He snatched the score sheet from Lydia.

"Your score for the six hands is only ninety-six." A gleam lit Ashtead's eyes. "Which awards the totals of both your scores, as well as the hundred point bonus for the top score, to Eddie."

"I am as well aware of that as you," sneered Kennilworth. "Another deck, man," he snapped at Marmaduke.

Ashtead stopped him with an upraised hand. "Let us settle the bets between each game." His steely gaze rested on Kennilworth. "I feel certain you will see the wisdom of that, Captain."

Kennilworth dragged out his purse with ill grace. And there came the bills, a little over three thousand pounds. Eddie took them with trembling hands, then passed them to Lydia to act as her banker. Marmaduke prepared and dealt the next hand, and Lydia, her expression intent, sat with pen ready to record the scoring for the declarations.

Kennilworth glared at his cards, then at Ashtead. "Having so great an audience is putting me off my game."

"Do you always whine so, or is it only when you are losing?" asked Marmaduke with polite interest.

"Consider it a truer test of your abilities to play under adverse conditions," suggested Ashtead.

At the end of the sixth hand of this second game, Eddie again found herself the winner, but by a much narrower margin, awarding her barely sixteen hundred pounds. Still, in this very short amount of time, she had recovered almost five thousand pounds. Another hour or so of play, and she might be able to walk away from this table and never sit down to piquet again.

Might, she reminded herself. She must maintain her concentration. Kennilworth was a dangerous opponent, and might prove especially so when cornered. Already his carefully cultivated calm had collapsed, and perspiration beaded his brow. Still, at the end of the next game, she had won back the vast sum lost by Marmaduke.

"Satisfied?" Kennilworth demanded through clenched teeth.

Eddie's gaze drifted to the impressive pile of bills held by a glowing Lydia. "Yes," she declared. She started to rise.

"Well, I am not," Kennilworth declared. He glared at Ashtead. "You have achieved your purpose, have you not? You have assured she held the proper cards. Now let us have a game where the deck is not arranged for her." He turned back to Eddie. "Or are you afraid to play against me when someone other than your uncle deals?"

Eddie stiffened. "I am not in the least bit afraid."

Marmaduke, who had taken a moment to work out the implication of the captain's words, stiffened. "Damme, the man's calling me a cheat! I have a good mind to draw his cork!"

"Pray, not in my aunt's drawing room," protested Lydia. "He is not worth the effort."

"No, I suppose he's not," Marmaduke agreed, though with a touch of regret.

"So you will play me?" Kennilworth's gaze fixed on Eddie, his eyes gleaming.

"Go ahead," said Ashtead. "The fellow obviously still needs a lesson."

"Give him a pack, Uncle Marmaduke," Eddie said.

Kennilworth broke it open, then with an exclamation of disgust swept the cards from their last hand aside. Marmaduke absently gathered and shuffled them, all the while his gaze remaining riveted on Kennilworth. The man's cold smile flashed. "Do you not like the odds when you are not in control?" he asked.

"Oh, I have implicit faith in your ability to control the cards," Marmaduke assured him.

The captain's complexion darkened, but he made no reply. He finished shuffling, dealt, and Eddie found herself running a rapid finger over the edges of each card as she sorted it. No, he hadn't had a chance to notch any of them. So why did he want this last game? That he intended to win back a sizable portion of the amount he had just lost, she could not doubt. But how did he expect to do it?

The first hand went easily to Eddie. Almost too easily. It made her even more anxious. Kennilworth dealt again, another new deck provided by Marmaduke, and Eddie once more checked the edges. Nothing.

Kennilworth coughed, then drew out his handkerchief and coughed again. Ashtead went to the sideboard and poured him a glass of wine, which the man accepted with the first signs of pleasure he had shown since entering the drawing room. "So it is to be a civilized evening after all," he said, and took a sip.

He collected his cards; Eddie played to his lead and

took the trick. Kennilworth coughed again, hesitated, started to draw out one card, then selected another. As he tossed it onto the table, Ashtead's hand shot out, grasped the captain's arm, and shook it. Three cards fell from the cuff of the captain's sleeve.

Lydia's gasp broke the stunned silence.

"He's concealing cards!" Marmaduke exclaimed, outraged.

"The man's a cheat!" Jacoby, his voice dripping disgust, left his post by the door and strode forward, his brow darkening.

Ashtead still held Kennilworth's arm against the table, his gaze on the man's flushed countenance. "Lydia, how stands the score?"

Lydia checked her paper. "There are only twelve points between them, with Eddie ahead."

"Her winnings?"

"About eight thousand, seven hundred pounds."

Ashtead nodded. "I believe we will finish this game."

The color drained from Kennilworth's face. He straightened, glaring around at them all, but the play proceeded. At the end of the sixth hand, Lydia held ten thousand, one hundred pounds for Eddie, along with the captain's vowel for eight hundred more.

"Not that I suppose you will ever see it," Ashtead said as he scanned the slip of paper. He turned back to Kennilworth. "We must thank you for a most interesting evening."

Kennilworth glared at him. "Do you mean you will now permit me to leave?"

Ashtead gave him his best innocent smile. "When did we ever constrain you to remain?"

"Damn you," breathed Kennilworth. "I should call you out for this."

"You haven't the courage," said Jacoby.

"At least I don't dangle after wealthy widows"—the captain shot a malevolent glance at Lydia—"even if they do welcome all comers to their beds."

As a parting shot, it was pretty weak, but it provoked considerable action. Ashtead sprang to his feet, knocking over his chair, but Jacoby moved even swifter. He grabbed Kennilworth by the lapels, dragged him from his seat, then landed him a facer that sent him sprawling. He stood over him, thoughtfully rubbing his bruised knuckles.

"Excellent form." Marmaduke nodded in surprised approval. "Must spend some time at Jackson's between his plays," he added to Eddie.

"William," breathed Lydia. She rushed to his side, grasping his right hand between hers to examine it. The gaze she raised to his held utter wonderment.

Jacoby turned his hand to clasp hers, then drew her close, apparently oblivious to the others in the room. As Eddie watched in relief, he gathered Lydia, unprotesting, into his arms and kissed her.

Ashtead grinned at this treatment of his sister. "I think they will do better alone for a bit," he said softly.

Kennilworth had risen to his knees, and knelt there, shaking his head as if to clear it. Ashtead grabbed him by the elbow and dragged him upright and out of the room. Marmaduke, beaming, offered Eddie his arm and led her out in state.

Mrs. Winslow stood in the doorway of the salon, one hand to her ample breast, watching wide-eyed as Ashtead propelled the captain down the hall. At the door, he turned the man to face him, holding both lapels. "I believe it would be best to absent yourself from society for a good length of time. You might find the clime in

Italy to be beneficial to your health. If you take my point?"

Kennilworth nodded, then winced. With tentative fingers he probed the jaw where Jacoby's punishing fist had landed. Ashtead opened the door, and Kennilworth, not standing upon ceremony, departed.

Mrs. Winslow looked from Ashtead's set face to Marmaduke's expansive grin. "Will you please tell me what has occurred?" she demanded.

Marmaduke's grin broadened even more. "It was beyond anything, my dear Mrs. Winslow. Beyond anything. A pleasure to behold." He took her arm and led her back into the salon, winked over his shoulder at Eddie, and closed the door behind him.

Which left Eddie facing Ashtead. He strode up to her with purposeful gait, and instinctively she drew back until she bumped into a pier table placed inconveniently against the wall. "He—he will undoubtedly give her a highly colorful account of the evening's proceedings," she tried.

"Undoubtedly." He spoke the word as if he kept his voice under strict control.

"I—I never would have expected such decisive action from Sir William," she hurried on.

"He can be roused when it truly matters."

"Your sister—"

"Quit trying to divert me." He came to a halt, glowering down at her. "You will kindly tell me what the devil you thought you were doing, not telling me about this scheme of yours."

She didn't want a fight with him. She was tired, and the fears and worries and emotions of the evening had taken a heavy toll. She struggled against a terrible desire to burst into tears. She countered this by feeding her indignation at his attack, and glared back at him. "And you will tell me what the—what you are about assuming you have any right to know what I do!"

"In case it has slipped your mind, you invited him in my name. That should give me some right."

Hot color flamed in her face as the undeniable truth of his words sank home. "I—I beg your pardon." They fell silent. He still looked at her; she could feel his steady regard. She studied the toes of her slippers.

"You have won your competence." He made it a simple statement, devoid of any overtones.

"Yes." She still couldn't quite believe it, that she had achieved her goal, fulfilled the wish agreement she had made with Xanthe. She was safe, she need never rely on anyone ever again. So why must she feel so depressed?

"What will you do?" Again, his voice sounded neutral, amazingly non-combative.

Suddenly, all she wanted was to escape, to go so far away she would never have to see any of these people ever again. These people she had come to care for, to love— Only Ashtead didn't want her, and to stay near him, near his family, would be too painful to bear. "I want to leave Brighton as soon as possible," she declared, sinking beneath the growing weight of her misery.

"I am afraid I have been guilty of meddling." Still no trace of emotion sounded in his voice.

She looked up to find his countenance equally unreadable. "Aren't you always?" she tried.

He ignored her weak attempt at humor. "Two weeks ago I spoke to a solicitor here and asked him to have someone look about for a suitable cottage nearby. I thought you might like to remain in the vicinity, since you have made a number of friends here. And because you enjoy the theater so much."

He paused, but she found she couldn't speak, couldn't command her voice to express the tangled web of conflicting emotions his words elicited.

"They have found one that sounds perfect. If you should like, I will take you to see it tomorrow."

She nodded. A cottage of her own, within visiting distance of the amenities of Brighton. She should be soaring with delight. Instead, her spirits sank to a new low.

And it was because he was actually *helping* her to her independence. She realized it with a rush, all the hopes she had cherished, against all odds, against all reason. Deep within her she had longed for this moment, when she would stand before him, free of the shackling ties her lack of fortune imposed on her. And in her longings, he had asked her to join with him, not as his dependent, but as his free and equal wife. And instead he had found her a cottage. He neither needed her nor wanted her. And she, contrary soul that she was, wanted him desperately.

This might well be the only time she ever rode in his curricle, the only time she ever sat behind these perfectly matched grays, pressed close against him. Xanthe, on her other side, gazed out over the hedgerows, fulfilling her role of chaperon. Every once in awhile a slight tremor of amusement rippled through the fairy at some joke or secret pleasure she did not see fit to share. It depressed Eddie even more.

They traversed a beautiful lane, lined along one side with elms and a yew hedge. Some great manor lay just beyond them; she could just catch glimpses of a distant gabled roof and chimney stacks as they played hide and seek with the leafy branches. A light breeze fanned her cheeks, and very little dust blew up from the road. Everything seemed just a bit too pleasant, too perfect, to be real. Eddie cast a suspicious glance at Xanthe. She *thought* she'd heard a suspicious humming right after they set forth that morning.

They turned off the lane onto a narrower track, lined with rose hedges run wild. Eddie's breath caught in her throat at sight of the multitudinous blossoms, the pinks and reds and yellows and whites that tumbled amongst each other, filling the rampant vines. And they seemed to go on forever. She'd never seen a road so lovely. Definitely, this had to be Xanthe's doing, trying to make her as happy as possible with what would likely be her future home. If so, she could only hope the spell would last into the dreary years that loomed ahead.

A wrought-iron gate, which had obviously undergone recent repairs, rose up on one side. Someone had cut back the ivy and roses that clung to it, revealing gleaming hinges. Ashtead drew his pair to a halt, and the tiger, who had perched up behind, sprang to the freshly raked gravel of the drive and ran to throw the gate wide. Ashtead gave his cattle the office.

They passed under a rose-covered archway and made an immediate sharp turn, which brought a small Tudor cottage into view. A soft gasp of delight escaped Eddie at the sight of the mullioned windows, the ivy and roses climbing the walls, the wild gardens and the tiny stable, with housing for no more than two horses and a single cart or carriage. The tiger sprinted to the grays' heads, and Ashtead jumped down, then held out his hands to assist Eddie.

She accepted his help, and the touch of his fingers

clasping hers drove all other thought from her mind. For a moment she returned his clasp, breathing in the scent of roses and lavender and honeysuckle and leather, her vision filled with nothing but his rough cut features. Her heart beat rapidly. This would be a memory frozen forever in time for her, to be taken out and relived during the long, empty evenings that stretched ahead of her. Then she was on the ground beside him, and he walked around the vehicle to help Xanthe.

With an effort, Eddie dragged her gaze from his back to once more study the cottage. Xanthe must have had a hand in its choosing. Her vague thoughts about the home she would one day occupy matched this too closely for chance. Except she would change the stepping stones along that walkway, and plant moss around them instead of the gravel. And a trellised arbor over there, with a bench on which to sit.

Ashtead took her elbow, and she looked up to meet his serious gaze. "Does it please you?"

"Yes." She didn't care if he meant his touch or the overgrown garden. Her gaze rested on his face, but already he looked away, toward the house to which he led her.

She forced her attention back to the low structure. She would hang a lace curtain in that window near the door. She could do whatever she chose, for she would be her own mistress. She could rise in the morning when she wished, take her meals when she fancied them, plant every inch of this wild garden in any manner that pleased her. The thought brought conflicting emotions, which she shoved aside. Not now. Let her examine this possible home free from regrets.

A comfortable sitting room, a small but adequate dining room, and a well-appointed kitchen comprised the

Janice Bennett

ground floor. An oak staircase led the way to two surprisingly spacious bedchambers, with windows overlooking both gardens. Eddie wandered from room to room, picturing herself living here. But try as she might, the hazy outline of an older female companion kept fading before the image of Ashtead sitting in a large chair before the hearth; With a sleepy spaniel at the feet he stretched out to meet the fire's warmth. She closed her eyes, but the image only grew sharper.

She turned to the dining room, and there she could see him sitting at a linen-covered table on which stood a triple-branched silver candelabrum, its white candles burning as he drank a glass of deep ruby wine from a crystal goblet. Dreams, she told herself in disgust. She would not be able to afford the luxuries of fine crystal and silver. Nor would she enjoy the luxury of Ashtead's companionship.

She returned to the salon to stare into the garden. A rustic bench now stood in the position she'd imagined. Xanthe, redecorating, obviously enjoying herself.

A booted footstep sounded behind her, but she didn't need to hear it to know that Ashtead had entered the room. She resonated to his mere presence, knew the scent of the lotion he used after shaving. It would haunt her, come back at odd moments, to remind her of him long after he'd left her life for good.

"What do you think?" he asked. His tone sounded neutral, as if he didn't care one way or the other whether it pleased her.

"It is exactly what I wanted." Yes, wanted. In the past tense. Until recently, she could have imagined no more perfect home for herself. But now she wanted something else. She wanted Ashtead, as aggravating and infuriating as he was. She loved him, and even here, in these near-perfect surroundings, she could not envision herself happy without him.

He came forward to stand at her side. "You will take it then?" Still, no trace of emotion, of interest, sounded in his voice. He had nothing at stake here. They might have argued, they might have laughed together, they might have spent the last two months coming to know one another, but in the end, his sole concern was to see her settled, one more obligation off his hands.

A fine mist stung her eyes. "How soon can I take possession of it?" She could not keep the catch from her voice, but doubted he would notice.

He cast a quick glance at her. "Something is troubling you. Do not feel obliged to take it because I found it for you. I will not be the least offended if you say it will not suit."

She shook her head. "I could be very happy here." At least she could if he chose to share it with her.

His gaze remained on her. "Is it leaving Brighton?"

"I will miss some of the people I have come to know."

"And you will worry about your disreputable uncle, is that it? I can relieve your mind on that score. My Aunt Hester has informed me she intends to marry him."

She looked up, startled. "He actually asked her? I had thought—I had hoped— But Uncle Marmaduke is so very accustomed to doing just as he pleases, I feared he would never bring himself up to scratch."

A touch of amusement lit Ashtead's eyes. "My aunt is a formidable opponent, though you would never guess it from her demeanor. She will make him extremely comfortable, and at the same time curb his tendencies toward the gaming table. I doubt he will realize she is influencing him in the least."

"And Lydia will marry Sir William. How very happy everyone will be."

"Except me." Ashtead's voice retained that calm, controlled tone.

Sudden hope sparked in Eddie, but she didn't dare permit it to fan to a flame. She swallowed, forcing herself to match the detached note in his voice. "You will have Grandfather's fortune, without any strings attached to it. You will be able to manage the estates and the charities exactly as you should wish."

"Not quite."

She turned to him, dismayed, her concern tearing apart her carefully controlled calm. "Has Grandfather gone back on his word? Oh, Ashtead, and I have been the cause—"

"No!" He caught her hands. He studied her face for a long moment, and a muscle tugged at the corner of his mouth. "It is just that without the greatest love of my heart at my side, my life will be very bleak." Her heart beat hard and fast, pounding in her ears.

"The—" She broke off, unable to let herself believe.

"Without you," he said softly, and drew her close.

She went as if in a dream, feeling the soft wool of his coat as his arms encircled her, drawing her against his broad chest. The smoothness of his chin and jaw pressed against her forehead as one powerful hand stroked her hair.

"You've earned your independence," he said. Constraint still sounded in his voice. "You will have your own cottage. You can escape from me any time you want. But could you not consider marrying me? You can keep the cottage, know that you are not tied to me by any bonds."

She shook her head, and found herself speaking into

the elaborate folds of his neckcloth. "But I am. I always will be. By love."

His hold on her tightened, to the imminent peril of her ribs. "My dearest life," he breathed, and his mouth sought hers in a kiss that demanded her very soul.

Independence—the hazy thought swirled through her mind as her sensations took over—was vastly overrated.

Epilogue

Xanthe sat cross-legged on a cushion of midnight-blue velvet, embroidered all around with tiny stars, moons, and candles. Sunlight streamed in through the mullioned pane of the Tudor cottage's bedchamber window, casting a lacy reflection across the waters of her mirrored bowl. Titus curled on a soft golden cushion across from her, his huge fluff of a tail dangling in midair. From outside came the dulcet song of a lark that perched on a branch near the window.

Xanthe passed her hand over the bowl; the shallow waters stirred, then settled, reflecting the image of the room below. Ashtead sat on the cottage's small sofa, with Eddie cradled on his lap, her head resting on his shoulder. His lips brushed her brow, and she looked up, meeting his smiling eyes with a gaze of pure love. He responded in the only possible manner: He drew her even closer and kissed her once more.

With a nod of satisfaction, Xanthe set the waters rippling, allowing them their solitude. "It will be time to leave soon," she informed Titus.

One of the cat's ears twitched.

"Enjoyed it, have you? So have I. But I admit I'm looking forward to a holiday amid my herbs and flowers."

Titus blinked and emitted a *myap* noise.

Xanthe regarded the huge feline with exasperation. Of course there are flowers and herbs here. And she will plant many more during their frequent stays."

Titus opened his mouth in a soundless meow.

"A retreat for them, to escape all the demands on their attention. He will be a marquis, remember, and in less than two years' time."

Again, the tail twitched. "Yes, of course she reconciles with her grandfather. He is a stubborn old man, and he can be very foolish at times, but he loves her dearly and has already remembered that fact. He will live long enough to see his first great-grandson. What? Oh, two sons and three daughters. And you wondered why they would be so grateful for a retreat where they can be alone together. Between their own children and Lydia's and Sir William's brood, they shall be delightfully busy, and dear Eddie will have all the love and laughter and companionship she has ever wanted. And then there is always the cottage when she needs a moment of independence."

Titus regarded her with sleepy eyes.

"Yes, of course we'll stay for the wedding. All three weddings, for we cannot ignore Lydia and her Sir William, or Marmaduke and Hester Winslow. What a delight they all will be. And then . . ." Her voice faded away. Humming softly, she floated to the window and gazed out over the garden, across the roses, past the hedge.

A long, peaceful rest. But after that? She closed her eyes, and the image of a hearth rose in her mind, of fire crackling merrily around three small logs arranged in the grate. Yes, and then. There would always be another fairy godchild she could help. Her, mischievous eyes twinkled with their eternal enjoyment.

BOOK YOUR PLACE ON OUR WEBSITE AND MAKE THE READING CONNECTION!

We've created a customized website just for our very special readers, where you can get the inside scoop on everything that's going on with Zebra, Pinnacle and Kensington books.

When you come online, you'll have the exciting opportunity to:

- View covers of upcoming books
- Read sample chapters
- Learn about our future publishing schedule (listed by publication month *and author*)
- Find out when your favorite authors will be visiting a city near you
- Search for and order backlist books from our online catalog
- Check out author bios and background information
- Send e-mail to your favorite authors
- Meet the Kensington staff online
- Join us in weekly chats with authors, readers and other guests
- Get writing guidelines
- AND MUCH MORE!

Visit our website at
http://www.zebrabooks.com